Sharing the Beauty of China 中华优秀传统文化传承发展工程支持项目

汉英对照 Chinese-English

唐诗与唐画
SELECTED POEMS AND PAINTINGS OF THE TANG DYNASTY

Translated by Xu Yuanchong

许渊冲 译

图书在版编目（CIP）数据

唐诗与唐画：汉英对照 / 许渊冲译．—— 北京：五洲传播出版社，2019.5
（中华之美）
ISBN 978-7-5085-4168-6

Ⅰ．①唐… Ⅱ．①许… Ⅲ．①唐诗－选集－汉、英②中国画－作品集－中国－唐代 Ⅳ．① I222.742 ② J222.42

中国版本图书馆 CIP 数据核字 (2019) 第 080164 号

"中华之美"丛书

主　　编　陈陆军
出 版 人　荆孝敏

唐诗与唐画（汉英对照）

译　　者　许渊冲
责任编辑　王　峰
助理编辑　王　玮
版式设计　殷金花
制　　版　北京紫航文化艺术有限公司
出版发行　五洲传播出版社
地　　址　北京市海淀区北三环中路 31 号生产力大楼 B 座 6 层
邮　　编　100088
发行电话　010-82005927，010-82007837
网　　址　http://www.cicc.org.cn，http://www.thatsbooks.com
印　　刷　深圳市彩美印刷有限公司
版　　次　2019 年 7 月第 1 版第 1 次印刷
开　　本　155mm×230mm　1/16
印　　张　15.5
字　　数　159 千
定　　价　146.00 元

共享中华之美
——"中华之美"丛书序

"文化是一个国家、一个民族的灵魂。"要了解中国,自然也离不开中国文化。中华民族五千多年文明历史所孕育的中华优秀传统文化,积淀了丰富多样的、弥足珍贵的民族精神财富,古典诗词是其中的瑰宝。

中国在历史上是一个"诗歌的国度",每个历史年代都留下了丰硕的诗歌成果,其中不少名篇名句,脍炙人口,传诵至今。中国古典诗词以其精炼优美的语言、丰富真挚的情感、含蓄委婉的意境,传唱千古而不衰,滋养着世代中国人的心灵。它们传递着中国人独特的思想智慧和艺术审美内涵,承载着中华民族的精神追求、人文价值和生命力量,是中华传统文化的精髓。

"中华之美"丛书选取的这些作品,是三千年来有代表性的中国优秀诗篇。中国古典诗词注重抒情、写景,善于表现各种复杂细微的情感。古代诗词中的优秀之作往往写得富于形象性和音乐性。我曾经提出,翻译是"美化之艺术",提出译作要追求意美、音美、形美"三美"。通过优秀的译作,将这些中华优秀诗作介绍给世界上更广大的读者,是我的心愿。

中国古典诗词善于表现自然之美及人与自然的融合。诗和画号称姊妹艺术,所以中国古人常说"诗中有画,画中有诗"。"中华之美"丛书精选了各个历史时代的中国经典画作，与诗词作品及相关历史背景有机结合起来，体现形神兼备、情景交融的中华美学追求。

英国诗人艾略特说过："个人的才智有限，文化的力量无穷。"21世纪是全球化的世纪。新世纪的新人不但应该了解全球的文化，而且应该使本国文化走向世界，成为全球文化的一部分，使世界文化更加灿烂辉煌。

近年来，中国古典诗词热在海内外不断升温，不仅激发了中国人对中华传统文化的热爱之情，也在许多海外人士尤其海外青少年心中埋下了中国文化的种子。衷心希望"中华之美"丛书能够帮助更多海外读者增进对中国文化的了解，让读者在审美过程中获得愉悦、感受中华文化魅力，使读者对中华文化"知之，好之，乐之"，共享中华之美。

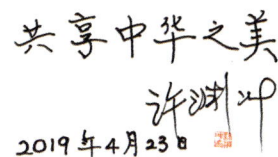

共享中华之美
许渊冲
2019年4月23日

PREFACE TO THE *SHARING THE BEAUTY OF CHINA* SERIES

Xu Yuanchong

"Culture is the soul of a country and its people." To better understand China, it is only natural to want to know more about the diverse and rich Chinese culture accumulated in a history of more than 5,000 years. Reading and enjoying classical poetry of China is indeed one of the shortcuts in this regard as well as a great joy for many.

Historically, China was a "country of poetry". Every historical period has left beautiful poems, many of which are well-known and continue to be recited so far. Chinese classical poetry, known for its refined and beautiful language, is concise but cherishes an implicit and euphemistic mood, striking a responsive chord among Chinese. These poems show their ideological wisdom, cultural pursuits and humanistic values.

Classical poems form an unbroken line considered to be the cream of poetry created in the past 3,000 years. All of them pay high attention to lyricism and scenery, expressing various complex and subtle emotions. Since classical Chinese poetry represent the combination of beauty in sense, sound and form, anyone seeking to translate them needs to try to reproduce the "three beauties" of the original. It is my wish to see a vivid materialization of this theory in doing translation work, because I strongly believe this theory has profound historical and cultural foundations.

Chinese classical poetry is good at expressing the beauty of nature and the integration of human emotions and nature. In the eyes of the Chinese, poetry and painting are close companions in the art world, so they often say, "There are 'paintings' in poetry, and there are 'poems' in paintings." The *Sharing the Beauty of China* series selects the best of the Chinese classical paintings created in various historical periods, combined with poems and related historical background in an organic way, that embody the pursuit of Chinese aestheticism with both form and spirit and the blending of scenes.

Thomas Steams Eliot (1888-1965), the English poet, once said that individual intelligence is limited, but culture is infinite. In the 21st Century which is believed to be a century of globalization, people should not only understand global culture, but also make sure their own culture is made available to the world, thus becoming a part of the global culture, and adding luster to the world culture.

Recent years have seen increasing popularity of Chinese classical poetry at home and abroad. This not only stimulates the Chinese people's love for their traditional culture, but also buries the seeds of Chinese culture in the hearts of many overseas people. I sincerely hope the *Sharing the Beauty of China* series can help more overseas readers of all age groups to gain pleasure and feel the charm of Chinese culture in the aesthetic process, enabling them to know and enjoy Chinese culture.

April 23, 2019

(Translated by Guozhen Wang)

目录
CONTENTS

王　勃
　　送杜少府之任蜀州 —— 001

贺知章
　　咏柳 —— 005
　　回乡偶书二首 —— 007

陈子昂
　　登幽州台歌 —— 008

张九龄
　　望月怀远 —— 011

张若虚
　　春江花月夜 —— 012

王　湾
　　次北固山下 —— 017

王　翰
　　凉州词 —— 021

王之涣
　　登鹳雀楼 —— 023
　　凉州词（其一）—— 026

孟浩然
　　过故人庄 —— 029
　　春晓 —— 030

Wang Bo
Farewell to Prefect Du — 001

He Zhizhang
The Willow — 005

Home-coming — 007

Chen Zi'ang
On the Tower at Youzhou — 008

Zhang Jiuling
Looking at the Moon and Longing for One Far Away — 011

Zhang Ruoxu
The Moon over the River on a Spring Night — 012

Wang Wan
Passing by the Northern Mountains — 017

Wang Han
Starting for the Front — 021

Wang Zhihuan
On the Stork Tower — 023

Out of the Great Wall — 026

Meng Haoran
Visiting an Old Friend's Cottage — 029

Spring Morning — 031

王昌龄

- 出塞 —— 032
- 闺怨 —— 034

王 维

- 山居秋暝 —— 037
- 使至塞上 —— 038
- 竹里馆 —— 041
- 相思 —— 043
- 九月九日忆山东兄弟 —— 044

李 白

- 峨眉山月歌 —— 047
- 望庐山瀑布 —— 048
- 望天门山 —— 051
- 静夜思 —— 052
- 黄鹤楼送孟浩然之广陵 —— 055
- 蜀道难 —— 057
- 行路难 —— 063
- 将进酒 —— 065
- 月下独酌 —— 070
- 梦游天姥吟留别 —— 072
- 宣州谢朓楼饯别校书叔云 —— 082
- 赠汪伦 —— 084
- 早发白帝城 —— 086

Wang Changling

- On the Frontier — 032
- Sorrow of a Young Bride in Her Boudoir — 034

Wang Wei

- Autumn Evening in the Mountains — 037
- On Mission to the Frontier — 039
- The Bamboo Hut — 041
- Love Seeds — 043
- Thinking of My Brothers on Mountain-climbing Day — 044

Li Bai

- The Moon over Mount Brow — 047
- The Waterfall in Mount Lu Viewed from Afar — 048
- Mount Heaven's Gate Viewed from Afar — 051
- Thoughts on a Tranquil Night — 052
- Seeing Meng Haoran off at Yellow Crane Tower — 055
- Hard is the Way to Shu — 058
- Hard is the Way of the World — 063
- Invitation to Wine — 068
- Drinking Alone under the Moon — 070
- Mount Skyland Ascended in a Dream — 077
- Farewell to Uncle Yun, Imperial Librarian, at Xie Tiao's Pavilion in Xuanzhou — 082
- To Wang Lun — 084
- Leaving the White Emperor Town at Dawn — 086

崔　颢
- 黄鹤楼 —— 089

常　建
- 题破山寺后禅院 —— 090

高　适
- 别董大 —— 095

刘长卿
- 逢雪宿芙蓉山主人 —— 096

杜　甫
- 望岳 —— 099
- 月夜 —— 100
- 春望 —— 104
- 石壕吏 —— 107
- 月夜忆舍弟 —— 110
- 蜀相 —— 113
- 客至 —— 115
- 春夜喜雨 —— 117
- 茅屋为秋风所破歌 —— 118
- 闻官军收河南河北 —— 123
- 绝句（两个黄鹂鸣翠柳）—— 125
- 旅夜书怀 —— 126
- 登岳阳楼 —— 128

Cui Hao

    Yellow Crane Tower — 089

Chang Jian

    A Buddhist Retreat behind an Old
    Temple in the Mountain — 090

Gao Shi

    Farewell to a Lutist — 095

Liu Zhangqing

    Seeking Shelter in Lotus Hill on a Snowy Night — 096

Du Fu

    Gazing on Mount Tai — 099

    A Moonlit Night — 100

    Spring View — 104

    The Pressgang at Stone Moat Village — 107

    Thinking of My Brother on a Moonlit Night — 110

    Temple of the Premier of Shu — 113

    For a Guest — 115

    Happy Rain on a Spring Night — 117

    My Cottage Unroofed by Autumn Gales — 118

    Recapture of the Regions North
    and South of the Yellow River — 123

    A Quatrain (Two golden orioles) — 125

    Mooring at Night — 127

    On Yueyang Tower — 129

岑　参
　　白雪歌送武判官归京 ——————————— 131
　　逢入京使 ——————————————————— 135

张　继
　　枫桥夜泊 ——————————————————— 138

韦应物
　　滁州西涧 ——————————————————— 141

孟　郊
　　游子吟 ———————————————————— 142

韩　愈
　　早春呈水部张十八员外 ———————————— 147

张　籍
　　节妇吟 ———————————————————— 148

刘禹锡
　　酬乐天扬州初逢席上见赠 ——————————— 151
　　乌衣巷 ———————————————————— 154

白居易
　　卖炭翁 ———————————————————— 156
　　长恨歌 ———————————————————— 160
　　琵琶行 ———————————————————— 175
　　赋得古原草送别 ——————————————— 191
　　钱塘湖春行 ————————————————— 193

柳宗元
　　江雪 ————————————————————— 196

Cen Shen

Song of White Snow in Farewell to Secretary
Wu Going Back to the Capital — 132

On Meeting a Messenger Going to the Capital — 135

Zhang Ji

Mooring by Maple Bridge at Night — 138

Wei Yingwu

On the West Stream at Chuzhou — 141

Meng Jiao

Song of the Parting Son — 142

Han Yu

Early Spring Written for Secretary Zhang Ji — 147

Zhang Ji

Reply of a Chaste Wife — 149

Liu Yuxi

Reply to Bai Juyi Whom I Meet for the
First Time at a Banquet in Yangzhou — 151

The Street of Mansions — 154

Bai Juyi

The Old Charcoal Seller — 159

The Everlasting Regret — 165

Song of a Pipa Player — 180

Grass on the Ancient Plain — 191

On Lake Qiantang in Spring — 193

Liu Zongyuan

Fishing in Snow — 196

崔　护
　　题都城南庄 —— 198
元　稹
　　离思 —— 201
贾　岛
　　访隐者不遇 —— 203
李　绅
　　悯农二首 —— 205
杜　牧
　　过华清宫 —— 207
　　江南春 —— 208
　　赤壁 —— 209
　　泊秦淮 —— 210
　　山行 —— 214
温庭筠
　　商山早行 —— 217
李商隐
　　锦瑟 —— 219
　　乐游原 —— 220
　　夜雨寄北 —— 222
　　无题（昨夜星辰昨夜风）—— 224
　　无题（相见时难别亦难）—— 227
　　嫦娥 —— 229

Cui Hu
- Written in a Village South of the Capital —— 198

Yuan Zhen
- Thinking of My Dear Departed —— 201

Jia Dao
- For an Absent Recluse —— 203

Li Shen
- The Peasants —— 205

Du Mu
- The Summer Palace —— 207
- Spring on the Southern Rivershore —— 208
- The Red Cliff —— 209
- Moored on River Qinhuai —— 210
- Going up the Hill —— 215

Wen Tingyun
- Early Departure —— 217

Li Shangyin
- The Sad Zither —— 219
- On the Plain of Tombs —— 220
- Written on a Rainy Night to My Wife in the North —— 222
- To One Unnamed (As last night twinkle stars) —— 224
- To One Unnamed (It's difficult) —— 227
- To the Moon Goddess —— 229

明皇幸蜀图（局部） 唐代 李昭道
Emperor Xuanzong's Journey to Shu (partial), Tang Dynasty, Li Zhaodao

王 勃 Wang Bo

送杜少府之任蜀州

城阙辅三秦，风烟望五津。
与君离别意，同是宦游人。
海内存知己，天涯若比邻。
无为在歧路，儿女共沾巾。

FAREWELL TO PREFECT DU

You leave the town walled far and wide
For mist-veiled land by riverside.
I feel on parting sad and drear,
For both of us are strangers here.
If you have friends who know your heart,
Distance cannot keep you apart.
At crossroads where we bid adieu,
Do not shed tears as women do!

Wang Bo (650?–676) was grouped together with Yang Jiong, Lu Zhaolin and Luo Binwang as the Four Paragons of the Early Tang Dynasty. Together with Lu Zhaolin, he tried to abandon the popular court poetry with meaningless figures of speech and squeamish refinement of words. Majority of his poems depict his personal life, but a few of them express his dissatisfaction with the political circle and imperial families. In terms of style, his poems are simple, but some are still flowery. His work *Wang Zi'an Anthology* which had been lost was compiled in the Ming Dynasty.

明皇幸蜀图（局部）
Emperor Xuanzong's Journey to Shu (partial)

江帆楼阁图（局部） 唐代 李思训
Sailboats and Pavilions in Vibrant Spring (partial), Tang Dynasty, Li Sixun

贺知章　He Zhizhang

咏柳

碧玉妆成一树高，
万条垂下绿丝绦。
不知细叶谁裁出？
二月春风似剪刀。

THE WILLOW

The slender tree is dressed in emerald all about;
A thousand branches droop like fringes made of jade.
But do you know by whom these slim leaves are cut out?
The wind of early spring is sharp as scissor blade.

He Zhizhang (659?–744?) was a poet and calligrapher in the early stage of prosperous Tang Dynasty. In addition to excelling in quatrain themed ritual and politics to serve the ruler, he was also known for his scenery and lyrics poems which featured unique fresh and natural style. Only 20 of his poems have been passed down to the generations, including the well-regarded *The Willow* and *Home-coming*.

游骑图（局部） 唐代 佚名
A Man Traveling around on Horseback (partial), Tang Dynasty, Anonymous

贺知章　He Zhizhang

回乡偶书二首

（一）

少小离家老大回，乡音无改鬓毛衰。
儿童相见不相识，笑问客从何处来。

（二）

离别家乡岁月多，近来人事半消磨。
惟有门前镜湖水，春风不改旧时波。

HOME-COMING

I

I left home young and not till old do I come back,
Unchanged my accent, my hair no longer black.
My children whom I meet do not know who am I.
"Where do you come from, sir?" they ask with beaming eye.

II

Since I left my homeland so many years have passed;
So much has faded away and so little can last.
Only in Mirror Lake before my oldened door
The vernal wind still ripples water as before.

陈子昂 Chen Zi'ang

登幽州台歌

前不见古人，

后不见来者。

念天地之悠悠，

独怆然而涕下。

ON THE TOWER AT YOUZHOU

Where are the great men of the past

And where are those of future years?

The sky and earth forever last;

Here and now I alone shed tears.

Chen Zi'ang (661–702) was generous in his youth and completed Jinshi level of imperial examination (means he was a successful candidate in the highest imperial examination) at the age of 24 years. He got Empress Wu's appreciation for his political opinions, which made him being accused of a rebel and put in prison. In light of being sent to safeguard fortress twice at the age of 26 and 36 years, he had some foresight in frontier fortress defence. At the age of 38 years, he returned to his hometown with his father who had resigned. In his poem, just like the poets in the Han and Wei dynasties, he kept an eye on the sentiment and real life issues, instead of rhetoric. He pioneered the new style of Tang poetry. His work includes *Chen Boyu Anthology*.

蛮夷执贡图 唐代 周昉
A Man in Ethnic Costume Paying Tribute, Tang Dynasty, Zhou Fang

韩熙载夜宴图（局部） 唐代 顾闳中
Banquet Scene in Han Xizai's Mansion (partial), Tang Dynasty, Gu Hongzhong

张九龄 Zhang Jiuling

望月怀远

海上生明月，天涯共此时。
情人怨遥夜，竟夕起相思。
灭烛怜光满，披衣觉露滋。
不堪盈手赠，还寝梦佳期。

LOOKING AT THE MOON AND LONGING FOR ONE FAR AWAY

Over the sea grows the moon bright;
We gaze on it far, far apart.
Lovers complain of long, long night;
They rise and long for the clear heart.
Candles blown out, fuller is light;
My coat put on, I'm moist with dew.
As I can't hand you moonbeams white,
I go to bed to dream of you.

Zhang Jiuling (678–740) was a prominent politician, poet and scholar, serving as chancellor during the reign of Emperor Xuanzong of Tang. He was proficient in five-character poems with simple words to express his inner feelings and ambitions. He played an important role in helping Tang poetry to abandon the Six Dynasties poem style of focusing on figures of speech. With vigorous style, his poems give attention to sentiments. *Qujian Anthology* is one of his works.

A Dancing Beauty, Tang Dynasty, Anonymous

张若虚　Zhang Ruoxu

春江花月夜

春江潮水连海平，海上明月共潮生。滟滟随波千万里，何处春江无月明？
江流宛转绕芳甸，月照花林皆似霰。空里流霜不觉飞，汀上白沙看不见。
江天一色无纤尘，皎皎空中孤月轮。江畔何人初见月？江月何年初照人？
人生代代无穷已，江月年年只相似。不知江月待何人，但见长江送流水。
白云一片去悠悠，青枫浦上不胜愁。谁家今夜扁舟子？何处相思明月楼？
可怜楼上月徘徊，应照离人妆镜台。玉户帘中卷不去，捣衣砧上拂还来。
此时相望不相闻，愿逐月华流照君。鸿雁长飞光不度，鱼龙潜跃水成文。
昨夜闲潭梦落花，可怜春半不还家。江水流春去欲尽，江潭落月复西斜。
斜月沉沉藏海雾，碣石潇湘无限路。不知乘月几人归？落月摇情满江树。

THE MOON OVER THE RIVER ON A SPRING NIGHT

In spring the river rises as high as the sea,
And with the river's tide uprises the moon bright.
She follows the rolling waves for ten thousand li;
Where'er the river flows, there overflows her light.
The river winds around the fragrant islet where

Zhang Ruoxu ((660?–720?) was traditionally grouped with He Zhizhang, Zhang Xu, and Bao Rong as the Four Poets of Central Wu, the Lower Yangtze region. Among his two existing poems, *The Moon over the River on a Spring Night* is still influential today. It uses *Yuefu* style, simple vocabularies and melodious rhyme to express the wanderers' strong yearnings for their lovers and contains rich life philosophies, different from the court poetry with so much rhetoric.

The blooming flowers in her light all look like snow.
You cannot tell her beams from hoar frost in the air,
Nor from white sand upon the Farewell Beach below.
No dust has stained the water blending with the skies;
A lonely wheellike moon shines brilliant far and wide.
Who by the riverside did first see the moon rise?
When did the moon first see a man by riverside?
Many generations have come and passed away;
From year to year the moons look alike, old and new.
We do not know tonight for whom she sheds her ray,
But hear the river say to its water adieu.
Away, away is sailing a single cloud white;
On Farewell Beach are pining away maples green.
Where is the wanderer sailing his boat tonight?
Who, pining away, on the moonlit rails would lean?
Alas! the moon is lingering over the tower;
It should have seen her dressing table all alone.
She may roll curtains up, but light is in her bower;
She may wash, but moonbeams still remain on the stone.
She sees the moon, but her husband is out of sight;
She would follow the moonbeams to shine on his face.
But message-bearing swans can't fly out of moonlight,
Nor letter-sending fish can leap out of their place.
He dreamed of flowers falling o'er the pool last night;
Alas! spring has half gone, but he can't homeward go.
The water bearing spring will run away in flight;
The moon over the pool will in the west sink low.
In the mist on the sea the slanting moon will hide;
It's a long way from northern hills to southern streams.
How many can go home by moonlight on the tide?
The setting moon sheds o'er riverside trees but dreams.

奕棋仕女图 唐代 佚名
A Beauty Playing Cheese, Tang Dynasty, Anonymous

江帆楼阁图（局部） 唐代 李思训
Sailboats and Pavilions in Vibrant Spring (partial), Tang Dynasty, Li Sixun

王 湾 Wang Wan

次北固山下

客路青山外，行舟绿水前。
潮平两岸阔，风正一帆悬。
海日生残夜，江春入旧年。
乡书何处达？归雁洛阳边。

PASSING BY THE NORTHERN MOUNTAINS

My boat goes by green mountains high
And passes through the river blue.
The banks seem wide at the full tide;
A sail with ease hangs in soft breeze.
The sun brings light born of last night;
New spring invades old year which fades.
Where can I send word to my end?
Homing wild geese, fly westward, please!

Poet Wang Wan lived in the north of the Tang Dynasty, but he often visited Jiangnan (south of Yangtze River) and wrote some works to chant the local beautiful mountains and lakes. Ten of his poems have been preserved and collected in *Quan Tang Shi (Complete Tang Poem)*. Among his poems, the most famous is *Passing By the Northern Mountain*, its third line that reads "The sun brings light born of last night; New spring invades old year" -is specifically very popular.

江帆楼阁图（局部）
Sailboats and Pavilions in Vibrant Spring (partial)

珠勒珊鞦狀驌驦如
茵芳草印蹄幾千里
休眠撩亂度雲霞
游字曲江芳郊无
物不堪畫令諸生歡
花影新挨鞭背就
聊立馬給他寄通

游骑图（局部） 唐代 佚名
A Man Traveling around on Horseback (partial), Tang Dynasty, Anonymous

王 翰 Wang Han

凉州词

葡萄美酒夜光杯，
欲饮琵琶马上催。
醉卧沙场君莫笑！
古来征战几人回？

STARTING FOR THE FRONT

With wine of grapes the cups of jade would glow at night;
Drinking to pipa songs, we are summoned to fight.
Don't laugh if we lay drunken on the battleground!
How many warriors ever came back safe and sound?

Born in a rich family, Wang Han lived a worldly and unselfconscious life, with specialties of singing, dancing and writing. Majority of his poems demonstrate such an idea that life is too short and people should enjoy it. His original work was lost.

宫苑图（局部） 唐代 佚名
Beautiful and Splendid Imperial Garden (partial), Tang Dynasty, Anonymous

王之涣　Wang Zhihuan

登鹳雀楼

白日依山尽，
黄河入海流。
欲穷千里目，
更上一层楼。

ON THE STORK TOWER

The sun along the mountain bows;
The Yellow River seawards flows.
You will enjoy a grander sight
If you climb to a greater height.

Wang Zhihuan (688–742) was a poet in the golden age of the Tang Dynasty, with his poems being recited by the professional entertainers. As a romantic poet, he was gifted in fortress poems. His masterpieces include *On the Stork Tower* and *Out of the Great Wall*.

宫苑图（局部）
Beautiful and Splendid Imperial Garden (partial)

峻岭溪桥图（局部） 唐代 郑虔
Majestic Mountains, Flowing Water and Small Bridges (partial), Tang Dynasty, Zheng Qian

王之涣　Wang Zhihuan

凉州词（其一）

黄河远上白云间，
一片孤城万仞山。
羌笛何须怨杨柳，
春风不度玉门关。

OUT OF THE GREAT WALL

The Yellow River rises to the white cloud;
The lonely town is lost amid the mountains proud.
Why should the Mongol flute complain no willows grow?
Beyond the Gate of Jade no vernal wind will blow.

江帆楼阁图（局部） 唐代 李思训
Sailboats and Pavilions in Vitality Spring (partial), Tang Dynasty, Li Sixun

孟浩然　Meng Haoran

过故人庄

故人具鸡黍，邀我至田家。
绿树村边合，青山郭外斜。
开轩面场圃，把酒话桑麻。
待到重阳日，还来就菊花。

VISITING AN OLD FRIEND'S COTTAGE

My friend's prepared chicken and rice;
I'm invited to his cottage hall.
Green trees surround the village nice;
Blue hills slant beyond city wall.
Windows open to field and ground;
O'er wine we talk of crops of grain.
On Double Ninth Day I'll come round
For the chrysanthemums again.

Meng Haoran (689–740) was a poet in the flouring Tang Dynasty. Despite pursuit of an official career in his youth, he was unwilling to be involved in sordid political scene of the times and chose to live in seclusion. In his poem, he was paralleled with Wang Wei and put natural world as the major topic of his poems to demonstrate his secluded life. *Meng Haoran Anthology* was left by him.

孟浩然　Meng Haoran

春晓

春眠不觉晓,
处处闻啼鸟。
夜来风雨声,
花落知多少!

丛篁集羽图（局部） 唐代 刁光胤（明摹本）
Birds in Bamboos (partial), Tang Dynasty, Diao Guangyin (copy of the Ming Dynasty)

Spring Morning

This spring morning in bed I'm lying,
Not to awake till birds are crying.
After one night of wind and showers,
How many are the fallen flowers!

王昌龄　Wang Changling

出塞

秦时明月汉时关,
万里长征人未还。
但使龙城飞将在,
不教胡马度阴山。

ON THE FRONTIER

The moon still shines on mountain passes as of yore.
How many guardsmen of the Great Wall are no more!

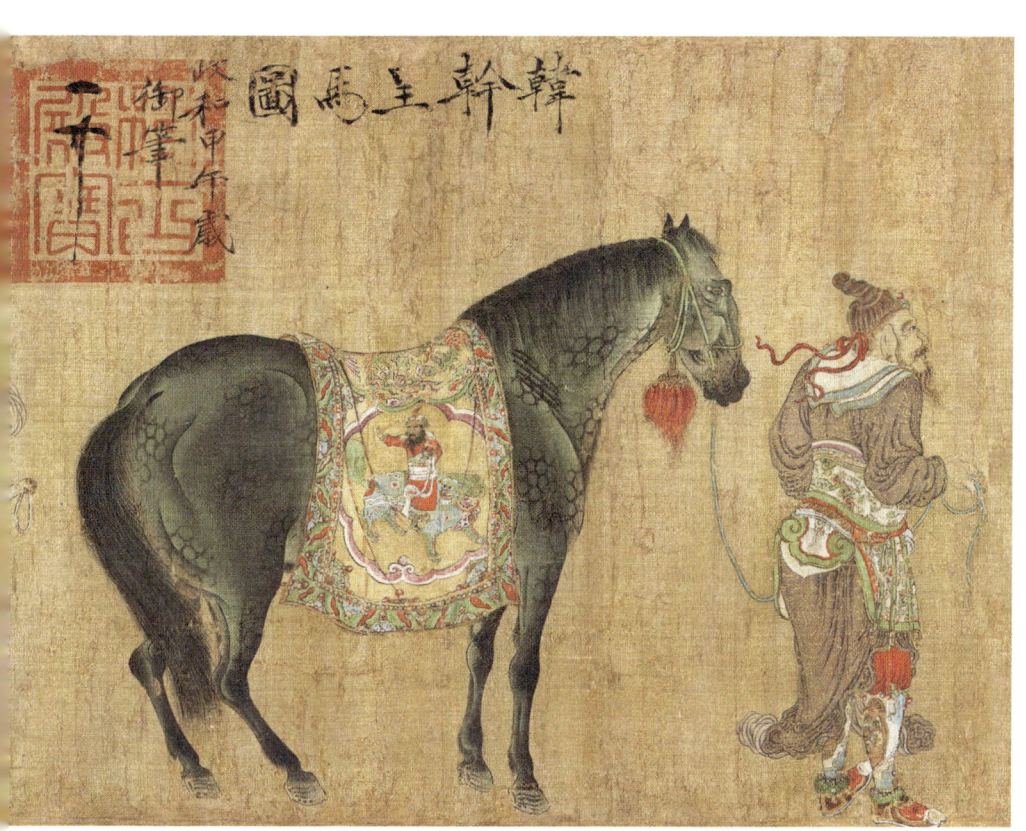

呈马图卷（局部）唐代 韩干
Horses Presented to Court (partial), Tang Dynasty, Han Gan

If the flying general were still there in command,
No hostile steeds would have dared to invade our land.

Wang Changling (?–756?) came from a poor background and relied on farming for livelihood in his childhood. At the age of 30 years, he completed the Jinshi level of imperial examination, but later, he was demoted and killed in a Lushan Rebellion, which was a devastating rebellion against the Tang Dynasty. He excelled in seven-character quatrains to depict the battles and magnificent landscape of the frontier regions, the sordid political environment as well as complain of disgraced court women. His work *Wang Changling Anthology* was compiled in the Ming Dynasty.

调琴啜茗图（局部） 唐代 佚名
Playing the Zither and Sipping the Tea (partial), Tang Dynasty, Anonymous

王昌龄　Wang Changling

闺怨

闺中少妇不知愁，
春日凝妆上翠楼。
忽见陌头杨柳色，
悔教夫婿觅封侯。

SORROW OF A YOUNG BRIDE IN HER BOUDOIR

The young bride in her boudoir does not know what grieves;
She mounts the tower, gaily dressed, on a spring day.
Suddenly seeing by roadside green willow leaves,
How she regrets her lord seeking fame far away!

调琴啜茗图（局部）
Playing the Zither and Sipping the Tea (partial)

王 维 Wang Wei

山居秋暝

空山新雨后，天气晚来秋。
明月松间照，清泉石上流。
竹喧归浣女，莲动下渔舟。
随意春芳歇，王孙自可留。

AUTUMN EVENING IN THE MOUNTAINS

After fresh rain in mountains bare
Autumn permeates evening air.
Among pine-trees bright moonbeams peer;
O'er crystal stones flows water clear.
Bamboos whisper of washer-maids;
Lotus stirs when fishing boat wades.
Though fragrant spring may pass away,
Still here's the place for you to stay.

Together with Meng Haoran, Wang Wei (699–761) was a famous poet. In addition to some frontier fortress poems written in his early years, he mainly pivoted to pastoral poems to advocate for a secluded life and Buddhist philosophies by natural sceneries. His poems are known for their vivid and expressive description. He was also in favour of music, painting and calligraphy. His work includes *Wang Youcheng Anthology*.

王 维 Wang Wei

使至塞上

单车欲问边,属国过居延。
征蓬出汉塞,归雁入胡天。
大漠孤烟直,长河落日圆。
萧关逢候骑,都护在燕然。

宫苑图（局部） 唐代 佚名
Beautiful and Splendid Imperial Garden (partial), Tang Dynasty, Anonymous

On Mission to the Frontier

A single carriage goes to the frontier;
An envoy crosses northwest mountains high.
Like tumbleweed I leave the fortress drear;
As wild geese I come 'neath Tartarian sky.
In boundless desert lonely smokes rise straight;
Over endless river the sun sinks round.
I meet a cavalier at the camp gate;
In northern fort the general will be found.

调琴啜茗图（局部） 唐代 佚名
Playing the Zither and Sipping the Tea (partial),
Tang Dynasty, Anonymous

王 维　Wang Wei

竹里馆

独坐幽篁里，
弹琴复长啸。
深林人不知，
明月来相照。

THE BAMBOO HUT

Sitting among bamboos alone,
I play my lute and croon carefree.
In the deep woods where I'm unknown,
Only the bright moon peeps at me.

韩熙载夜宴图（局部） 唐代 顾闳中
Banquet Scene in Han Xizai's Mansion (partial), Tang Dynasty, Gu Hongzhong

王 维　Wang Wei

相思

红豆生南国，
春来发几枝。
愿君多采撷，
此物最相思。

LOVE SEEDS

Red berries grow in southern land.
How many load in spring the trees?
Gather them till full is your hand;
They would revive fond memories.

王 维 Wang Wei

九月九日忆山东兄弟

独在异乡为异客,

每逢佳节倍思亲。

遥知兄弟登高处,

遍插茱萸少一人。

THINKING OF MY BROTHERS ON MOUNTAIN-CLIMBING DAY

Alone, a lonely stranger in a foreign land,
I doubly pine for my kinsfolk on holiday.
I know my brothers would, with dogwood spray in hand,
Climb up the mountain and miss me so far away.

宫阙图册 唐代 李思训
Bustling Imperial Palace, Tang Dynasty, Li Sixun

蓬莱飞雪图（局部） 唐代 杨升
Flowing Snow in Penglai (partial), Tang Dynasty, Yang Sheng

李 白 Li Bai

峨眉山月歌

峨眉山月半轮秋，
影入平羌江水流。
夜发清溪向三峡，
思君不见下渝州。

THE MOON OVER MOUNT BROW

The crescent moon looks like old Autumn's golden brow;
Its deep reflection flows with limpid water blue.
I'll leave the town on Clear Stream for three canyons now.
O Moon, how I miss you when you are out of view!

Li Bai (701–762) was a prominent romantic poet in the Tang Dynasty, and known as "Immortal Poet". He was comparable with Du Fu. He was very outgoing and kind and liked drinking wine, writing poems and making friends. With vigorous and bold style, his poems are known for rich imagination, smooth words as well as various and harmonious rhyme. Inspired by folk songs and myths, his works are colourful and romantic. *Li Taibai Anthology* was written by him.

明皇幸蜀图（局部） 唐代 李昭道
Emperor Xuanzong's Journey to Shu (partial), Tang Dynasty, Li Zhaodao

李 白 Li Bai

望庐山瀑布

日照香炉生紫烟，
遥看瀑布挂前川。
飞流直下三千尺，
疑是银河落九天。

THE WATERFALL IN MOUNT LU VIEWED FROM AFAR

The sunlit Censer Peak exhales incenselike cloud;
Like an upended stream the cataract sounds loud.
Its torrent dashes down three thousand feet from high
As if the Silver River fell from the blue sky.

江帆楼阁图（局部） 唐代 李思训
Sailboats and Pavilions in Vitality Spring (partial), Tang Dynasty, Li Sixun

李 白　Li Bai

望天门山

天门中断楚江开，
碧水东流至此回。
两岸青山相对出，
孤帆一片日边来。

MOUNT HEAVEN'S GATE VIEWED FROM AFAR

Breaking Mount Heaven's Gate, the great River rolls through;
Green billows eastward flow and here turn to the north.
From both sides of the River thrust out the cliffs blue;
Leaving the sun behind, a lonely sail comes forth.

蓬莱飞雪图（局部） 唐代 杨升
Flowing Snow in Penglai (partial), Tang Dynasty, Yang Sheng

李 白 Li Bai

静夜思

床前明月光，
疑是地上霜。
举头望明月，
低头思故乡。

THOUGHTS ON A TRANQUIL NIGHT

Before my bed a pool of light—
Can it be hoar-frost on the ground?
Looking up, I find the moon bright;
Bowing, in homesickness I'm drowned.

山水图 唐代 裴宽（传）
Landscapes, Tang Dynasty, Pei Kuan (purported)

李 白 Li Bai

黄鹤楼送孟浩然之广陵

故人西辞黄鹤楼,
烟花三月下扬州。
孤帆远影碧空尽,
唯见长江天际流。

SEEING MENG HAORAN OFF AT YELLOW CRANE TOWER

My friend has left the west where the Yellow Crane towers
For River Town veiled in green willows and red flowers.
His lessening sail is lost in the boundless blue sky,
Where I see but the endless River rolling by.

明皇幸蜀图（局部） 唐代 李昭道
Emperor Xuanzong's Journey to Shu (partial), Tang Dynasty, Li Zhaodao

李 白 Li Bai

蜀道难

噫吁嚱！危乎高哉！蜀道之难，难于上青天！
蚕丛及鱼凫，开国何茫然！
尔来四万八千岁，不与秦塞通人烟。
西当太白有鸟道，可以横绝峨眉巅。
地崩山摧壮士死，然后天梯石栈相钩连。
上有六龙回日之高标，下有冲波逆折之回川。
黄鹤之飞尚不得过，猿猱欲度愁攀援。
青泥何盘盘，百步九折萦岩峦。
扪参历井仰胁息，以手抚膺坐长叹。
问君西游何时还？畏途巉岩不可攀。
但见悲鸟号古木，雄飞雌从绕林间。
又闻子规啼夜月，愁空山。
蜀道之难，难于上青天，使人听此凋朱颜！
连峰去天不盈尺，枯松倒挂倚绝壁。
飞湍瀑流争喧豗，砯崖转石万壑雷。
其险也如此，嗟尔远道之人胡为乎来哉！
剑阁峥嵘而崔嵬，一夫当关，万夫莫开。
所守或匪亲，化为狼与豺。

朝避猛虎，夕避长蛇。

磨牙吮血，杀人如麻。

锦城虽云乐，不如早还家。

蜀道之难，难于上青天，侧身西望长咨嗟！

Hard is the Way to Shu

Oho! behold! how steep! how high!
The westward way is harder than to climb the sky.
Since the two pioneers
Put the kingdom in order,
Have passed forty eight thousand years,
And few have tried to pass its border.

御苑采莲图（局部） 唐代 李思训
Picking Lotus in Imperial Garden (partial), Tang Dynasty, Li Sixun

Only birds could fly o'er White Mountains in the west,
And up to Mount Brows' crest.
After the mountain crumbled and road-builders died,
A rocky path was hacked along the mountain side.
Above stand peaks too high for dragons to pass o'er;
Below the torrents run back and forth, churn and roar.
Even the golden crane can't fly across;
How to climb over, gibbons are at a loss.
What tortuous mountain path Green Mud Ridge faces!
Around the top we make nine turns each hundred paces.
Looking up breathless, I could touch the stars nearby;

明皇幸蜀图（局部） 唐代 李昭道
Emperor Xuanzong's Journey to Shu (partial), Tang Dynasty, Li Zhaodao

Beating my breast, I sink on the ground with a sigh.
When will you come back from this journey to the west?
How can you climb up dangerous path and mountain crest?
There you can hear on ancient trees but sad birds wail,
And see the male birds fly, followed by the female,
And hear home-going cuckoos weep
Beneath the moon in mountains deep.
The westward way is harder than to climb the sky.
On hearing this, your cheeks would lose their rosy dye.
Between the sky and peaks there seems less than a foot;
An old pine, head down, sticks into the cliff its root.
The cataracts and torrents vie in roaring loud;
Like thunder roll down frozen crags and boulders proud.
So dangerous these places are!
Alas! why should you come here from afar?
Rugged is the path between the cliffs so steep and high,
Guarded by one
And forced by none.
But disloyal guards
Might turn wolves and pards,
Man-eating tigers at daybreak
And at dusk blood- sucking serpent and snake.
You may find pleasure in the City of Brocade,
But it is better to go home, I am afraid.
The way to Shu is harder than to climb the sky,
I would turn westward and heave sigh on sigh.

长江积雪图（局部） 唐代 王维
Snow along the Yangtze River (partial), Tang Dynasty, Wang Wei

李 白 Li Bai

行路难

金樽清酒斗十千,玉盘珍羞直万钱。
停杯投箸不能食,拔剑四顾心茫然。
欲渡黄河冰塞川,将登太行雪满山。
闲来垂钓碧溪上,忽复乘舟梦日边。
行路难,行路难,多歧路,今安在?
长风破浪会有时,直挂云帆济沧海。

HARD IS THE WAY OF THE WORLD

Pure wine in golden cup costs ten thousand coppers, good!
Choice dish in a jade plate is worth as much, nice food!
Pushing aside my cup and chopsticks, I can't eat;
Drawing my sword and looking round, I hear my heart beat.
I can't cross Yellow River: ice has stopped its flow;
I can't climb Mount Taihang: the sky is blind with snow.
I poise a fishing pole with ease on the green stream
Or set sail for the sun like the sage in a dream.
Hard is the way, hard is the way.
Don't go astray! Whither today?
A time will come to ride the wind and cleave the waves;
I'll set my cloudlike sail to cross the sea which raves.

韩熙载夜宴图（局部） 唐代 顾闳中
Banquet Scene in Han Xizai's Mansion (partial), Tang Dynasty, Gu Hongzhong

李 白 Li Bai

将进酒

君不见黄河之水天上来，奔流到海不复回。
君不见高堂明镜悲白发，朝如青丝暮成雪。
人生得意须尽欢，莫使金樽空对月。
天生我材必有用，千金散尽还复来。
烹羊宰牛且为乐，会须一饮三百杯。
岑夫子，丹丘生，将进酒，杯莫停。
与君歌一曲，请君为我倾耳听。
钟鼓馔玉不足贵，但愿长醉不复醒。
古来圣贤皆寂寞，惟有饮者留其名。
陈王昔时宴平乐，斗酒十千恣欢谑。
主人何为言少钱？径须沽取对君酌。
五花马，千金裘，
呼儿将出换美酒，与尔同销万古愁。

韩熙载夜宴图（局部）
Banquet Scene in Han Xizai's Mansion (partial)

宴饮图 唐墓壁画 佚名
Banquet Scene, Mural in the Tang Tomb, Anonymous

INVITATION TO WINE

Do you not see the Yellow River come from the sky,
Rushing into the sea and ne'er come back?
Do you not see the mirrors bright in chambers high
Grieve o'er the snow-white hair though once silk-black?
When hopes are won, O drink your fill in high delight,
And never leave your wine-cup empty in moonlight!
Heaven has made us talents, we're not made in vain.
A thousand gold coins spent, more will turn up again.
Kill a cow, cook a sheep and let us merry be,
And drink three hundred cupfuls of wine in high glee!
Dear friends of mine,
Cheer up, cheer up!
I invite you to wine.
Do not put down your cup!
I will sing you a song, please hear,
O hear! Lend me a willing ear!
Do not care for bells and drums, rare dishes you take!
I only want to get drunk and never to wake.
How many great men were forgotten through the ages?

But great drinkers are more famous than sober sages.
The prince of Poets feast'd in his palace at will,
Drank wine at ten thousand a cask and laughed his fill.
Why should a host complain of money he is short?
To drink with you I will sell things of any sort.
My fur coat worth a thousand coins of gold
And my flower-dappled horse may be sold
To buy good wine that we may drown the woe age-old.

李 白 Li Bai

月下独酌

花间一壶酒，独酌无相亲。
举杯邀明月，对影成三人。
月既不解饮，影徒随我身。
暂伴月将影，行乐须及春。
我歌月徘徊，我舞影零乱。
醒时同交欢，醉后各分散。
永结无情游，相期邈云汉。

Drinking Alone under the Moon

Among the flowers, from a pot of wine
I drink without a companion of mine.
I raise my cup to invite the Moon who blends
Her light with my Shadow and we're three friends.
The Moon does not know how to drink her share;
In vain my Shadow follows me here and there.
Together with them for the time I stay,
And make merry before spring's spent away.
I sing and the Moon lingers to hear my song;

人物故事图册 唐代 阎立本（传）
Album of Figures and Stories, Tang Dynasty, Yan Liben (purported)

My Shadow's a mess while I dance along.
Sober, we three remain cheerful and gay;
Drunken, we part and each may go his way.
Our friendship will outshine all earthly love;
Next time we'll meet beyond the stars above.

李 白 Li Bai

梦游天姥吟留别

海客谈瀛洲,烟涛微茫信难求。
越人语天姥,云霓明灭或可睹。
天姥连天向天横,势拔五岳掩赤城。
天台四万八千丈,对此欲倒东南倾。
我欲因之梦吴越,一夜飞度镜湖月。
湖月照我影,送我至剡溪。
谢公宿处今尚在,渌水荡漾清猿啼。
脚著谢公屐,身登青云梯。
半壁见海日,空中闻天鸡。

海天旭日图（局部） 唐代 李昭道（宋摹本）
The Morning Sun over the Sea (partial), Tang Dynasty, Li Zhaodao (Copy of the Song Dynasty)

千岩万转路不定，迷花倚石忽已暝。
熊咆龙吟殷岩泉，栗深林兮惊层巅。
云青青兮欲雨，水澹澹兮生烟。
列缺霹雳，丘峦崩摧。
洞天石扉，訇然中开。
青冥浩荡不见底，日月照耀金银台。
霓为衣兮风为马，云之君兮纷纷而来下。
虎鼓瑟兮鸾回车，仙之人兮列如麻。
忽魂悸以魄动，恍惊起而长嗟。

海天旭日图（局部）
The Morning Sun over the Sea (partial)

海天旭日图（局部）
The Morning Sun over the Sea (partial)

惟觉时之枕席，失向来之烟霞。
世间行乐亦如此，古来万事东流水。
别君去兮何时还？
且放白鹿青崖间，须行即骑访名山。
安能摧眉折腰事权贵，使我不得开心颜！

Mount Skyland Ascended in a Dream — A Song of Farewell

Of fairy isles seafarers speak,
'Mid dimming mist and surging waves, so hard to seek.
Of Skyland southerners are proud,
Perceivable through fleeting or dispersing cloud.
Mount Skyland threatens heaven, massed against the sky,
Surpassing the Five Peaks and dwarfing Mount Red Town.
Mount Heaven's Terrace, five hundred thousand feet high,
Nearby to the southeast, appears crumbled down.
Longing in dreams for Southern Land, one night
I flew o'er Mirror Lake in moonlight.

猿马图（局部） 唐代 韩干
Apes and Horses in Leisure (partial), Tang Dynasty, Han Gan

My shadow's followed by moonbeams
Until I reach Shimmering Streams.
Where Hermitage of Master Xie can still be seen,
And clearly gibbons wail o'er rippling water green.
I put Xie's pegged boot
Each on one foot,
And scale the mountain ladder to blue cloud.
On eastern cliff I see
Sunrise at sea,
And in mid-air I hear sky cock crow loud.
The footpath meanders 'mid a thousand crags in the vale,
I'm lured by rocks and flowers when the day turns pale.
Bears roar and dragons howl and thunders the cascade;
Deep forests quake and ridges tremble: they're afraid.
From dark, dark cloud comes rain;
On pale, pale waves mists plane.
O lightning flashes
And thunder rumbles;
With stunning crashes

十六神骏图（局部） 唐代 韩干
16 Horses with Various Poses (partial), Tang Dynasty, Han Gan

Peak on peak crumbles.
The stone gate of a fairy cavern under
Suddenly breaks asunder.
So blue, so deep, so vast appears an endless sky,
Where sun and moon shine on gold and silver terraces high.
Clad in the rainbow, riding on the wind,
The lords of clouds descend in a procession long,
Their chariots drawn by phoenix disciplined,
And tigers playing for them a zither song,
Row upon row, like fields of hemp, immortals throng.
Suddenly my heart and soul stirred, I
Awake with a long, long sigh.
I find my head on pillow lie
And fair visions gone by.
Likewise all human joys will pass away
Just as east-flowing water of olden day.
I'll take my leave of you, not knowing for how long,
I'll tend a white deer among
The grassy slopes of the green hill
So that I may ride it to famous mountains at will.
How can I stoop and bow before the men in power
And so deny myself a happy hour!

李 白 Li Bai

宣州谢朓楼饯别校书叔云

弃我去者，昨日之日不可留。
乱我心者，今日之日多烦忧。
长风万里送秋雁，对此可以酣高楼。
蓬莱文章建安骨，中间小谢又清发。
俱怀逸兴壮思飞，欲上青天揽明月。
抽刀断水水更流，举杯销愁愁更愁。
人生在世不称意，明朝散发弄扁舟。

FAREWELL TO UNCLE YUN, IMPERIAL LIBRARIAN, AT XIE TIAO'S PAVILION IN XUANZHOU

What left me yesterday
Can be retained no more;
What troubles me today
Is the times I deplore.
For miles and miles the autumn breeze
Blows away the wild geese;
Let us drink our cups dry
In this pavilion high!

Beauty Painting, Tang Dynasty, Anonymous

The prince of poets wrote with those in Fairy Isle,
And Junior Xie had his clear and spirited style.
We have the same ideal to fly
Up to the moon in the blue sky.
But when we cut water with sword, still it will flow;
When we drink to lighten grief, heavier it will grow.
If in this world we cannot drown our sorrow,
Then sail a boat with loosened hair tomorrow!

蓬莱飞雪图（局部） 唐代 杨升
Flowing Snow in Penglai (partial), Tang Dynasty, Yang Sheng

李 白 Li Bai

赠汪伦

李白乘舟将欲行，
忽闻岸上踏歌声。
桃花潭水深千尺，
不及汪伦送我情！

To Wang Lun

I, Li Bai, sit aboard a ship about to go,
When suddenly on shore your farewell songs o'erflow.
However deep the Lake of Peach Blossoms may be,
It's not so deep, O Wang Lun! as your love for me.

李 白 Li Bai

早发白帝城

朝辞白帝彩云间,
千里江陵一日还。
两岸猿声啼不住,
轻舟已过万重山。

LEAVING THE WHITE EMPEROR TOWN AT DAWN

Leaving at dawn the White Emperor crowned with cloud,
I've sailed a thousand miles through canyons in a day.
With monkeys' sad adieus the riverbanks are loud;
My skiff has left ten thousand mountains far away.

猿马图（局部）唐代 韩干
Apes and Horses in Leisure (partial), Tang Dynasty, Han Gan

九成避暑图（局部）唐代 李思训
Imperial Summer Palace (partial), Tang Dynasty, Li Sixun

崔颢 Cui Hao

黄鹤楼

昔人已乘黄鹤去，此地空余黄鹤楼。
黄鹤一去不复返，白云千载空悠悠。
晴川历历汉阳树，芳草萋萋鹦鹉洲。
日暮乡关何处是？烟波江上使人愁。

YELLOW CRANE TOWER

The sage on yellow crane was gone amid clouds white.
To what avail is Yellow Crane Tower left here?
Once gone, the yellow crane will ne'er on earth alight;
Only white clouds still float in vain from year to year.
By sunlit river trees can be count'd one by one;
On Parrot Islet sweet green grass grows fast and thick.
Where is my native land beyond the setting sun?
The mist-veiled waves of River Han make me homesick.

Cui Hao (?–754) served as an official in the early Tang Dynasty and was upright and clever. At first, he wrote women-themed lyric poems, but later turned into frontier fortress poems with magnificent and vigorous in style. *Cui Hao Anthology* was compiled in the Ming Dynasty.

京畿瑞雪图（局部） 唐代 李思训
Snow Scene in the Capital City and Its Environs (partial), Tang Dynasty, Li Sixun

常 建　Chang Jian

题破山寺后禅院

清晨入古寺，初日照高林。
竹径通幽处，禅房花木深。
山光悦鸟性，潭影空人心。
万籁此俱寂，但余钟磬音。

A Buddhist Retreat behind an Old Temple in the Mountain

I come to the old temple at first light;
Only tree-tops are steeped in sunbeams bright.
A winding footpath leads to deep retreat;
The abbot's cell is hid' mid flowers sweet.
In mountain's aura flying birds feel pleasure;
In shaded pool a carefree mind finds leisure.
All worldly noises are quieted here;
I only hear temple bells ringing clear.

Chang Jian who didn't succeed in official career spent several years traveling to different places to enjoy beautiful sceneries and later lived in seclusion. In addition to writing frontier fortress poems, he often put a close eye on mountains and temples as the topics of his five-character poems, but a few of his works were preserved. He wrote *Chang Jian Anthology*.

京畿瑞雪图（局部）
Snow Scene in the Capital City and Its Environs (partial)

京畿瑞雪图（局部）
Snow Scene in the Capital City and Its Environs (partial)

高 适 Gao Shi

别董大

千里黄云白日曛，北风吹雁雪纷纷。
莫愁前路无知己，天下谁人不识君？

Farewell to a Lutist

Yellow clouds spread for miles and miles have veiled the day;
The north wind blows down snow and wild geese fly away.
Fear not you've no admirers as you go along!
There is no connoisseur on earth but loves your song.

Gao Shi (702?–765) served as government official in the Tang Dynasty. He and Cen Shen had roughly similar style in poem writing. Both were outstanding representatives of frontier fortress poems in the Tang Dynasty. Gao Shi's poems are of great momentum and magnificent, showcasing the vitality and prosperity of the Tang Dynasty in the golden times. He left *Gao Changshi Anthology*.

刘长卿　Liu Zhangqing

逢雪宿芙蓉山主人

日暮苍山远，
天寒白屋贫。
柴门闻犬吠，
风雪夜归人。

SEEKING SHELTER IN LOTUS HILL ON A SNOWY NIGHT

At sunset hillside village still seems far;
Cold and deserted the thatched cottages are.
At wicket gate a dog is heard to bark;
With wind and snow I come when night is dark.

Liu Zhangqing (?–786?) was a poet and politician in the Tang Dynasty, but there is still a relatively large current controversy on the dates of his birth and death. After passing the Jinshi level of imperial examination, he was appointed as a government official, but got framed and demoted several times. Therefore, most of his poems mostly demonstrate his frustration in career and separation from his friends by scenery description. Liu was especially skilful on writing poems with 5 characters. His work includes *Liu Suizhou Poetry Anthology*.

蓬莱飞雪图 唐代 杨升
Flowing Snow in Penglai, Tang Dynasty, Yang Sheng

春山行旅图 唐代 李昭道
Traveling in Spring Mountains, Tang Dynasty, Li Zhaodao

杜 甫 Du Fu

望岳

岱宗夫如何？齐鲁青未了。
造化钟神秀，阴阳割昏晓。
荡胸生层云，决眦入归鸟。
会当凌绝顶，一览众山小。

GAZING ON MOUNT TAI

O peak of peaks, how high it stands!
One boundless green o'erspreads two States.
A marvel done by Nature's hands,
O'er light and shade it dominates.
Clouds rise therefrom and lave my breast;
My eyes are strained to see birds fleet.
Try to ascend the mountain's crest:
It dwarfs all peaks under our feet.

Du Fu (712–770) was a follower of the Confucian ideology of "Benevolent Governance" and later quitted his job for being away from political turmoil. Popularly known as the "Poet Sage", he was the greatest of the Chinese poet, together with "Immortal Poet" Li Bai. His poems had historical significance and saw the evolution of the Tang Dynasty from wax to wane. He was proficient in ancient-form and regulated verses to display various styles, especially gloominess, having a profound influence on the development of Chinese classic poetry. He left Du *Gongbu Anthology*.

婴戏图（局部） 唐代 周昉
Babies Taking the Bathes (partial), Tang Dynasty, Zhou Fang

杜 甫 Du Fu

月夜

今夜鄜州月，闺中只独看。
遥怜小儿女，未解忆长安。
香雾云鬟湿，清辉玉臂寒。
何时倚虚幌，双照泪痕干？

A MOONLIT NIGHT

On the moon over Fuzhou which shines bright,
Alone you would gaze in your room tonight.
I'm grieved to think our little children are
Too young to yearn for their father afar.
Your cloudlike hair is moist with dew, it seems;
Your jade-white arms would feel the cold moonbeams.
O when can we stand by the windowside,
Watching the moon with tears already dried?

婴戏图（局部）
Babies Taking the Bathes (partial)

杜 甫 Du Fu

春望

国破山河在，城春草木深。
感时花溅泪，恨别鸟惊心。
烽火连三月，家书抵万金。
白头搔更短，浑欲不胜簪。

Spring View

On war-torn land streams flow and mountains stand;
In vernal town grass and weeds are o'ergrown.
Grieved o'er the years, flowers make us shed tears;
Hating to part, hearing birds breaks our heart.
The beacon fire has gone higher and higher;
Words from household are worth their weight in gold.
I cannot bear to scratch my grizzling hair;
It grows too thin to hold a light hairpin.

双骑图 唐代 韦偃
Two Men on Horsebacks, Tang Dynasty, Wei Yan

职贡图（局部） 唐代 阎立本
Envois from Tributary States of Tang Dynasty (partial), Tang Dynasty, Yan Liben

杜 甫　Du Fu

石壕吏

暮投石壕村，有吏夜捉人。
老翁逾墙走，老妇出门看。
吏呼一何怒！妇啼一何苦！
听妇前致词："三男邺城戍。
一男附书至，二男新战死。
存者且偷生。死者长已矣！
室中更无人，惟有乳下孙。
有孙母未去，出入无完裙。
老妪力虽衰，请从吏夜归。
急应河阳役，犹得备晨炊。"
夜久语声绝，如闻泣幽咽。
天明登前途，独与老翁别。

THE PRESSGANG AT STONE MOAT VILLAGE

I seek for shelter at nightfall.
What is the pressgang coming for?
My old host climbs over the wall;
My old hostess answers the door.
How angry is the sergeant's shout!
How bitter is the woman's cry!

I hear what she tries to speak out.
"I'd three sons guarding the town high.
One wrote a letter telling me
That his brothers were killed in war.
He'll keep alive if he can be;
The dead have passed and are no more.
In the house there is no man left,
Except my grandson in the breast
Of his mother, of all bereft;

职贡图（局部）
Envois from Tributary States of Tang Dynasty (partial)

She can't come out, in tatters dressed.
Though I'm a woman weak and old,
I beg to go tonight with you,
That I may serve in the stronghold
And cook morning meals as my due."
With night her voices fade away;
I seem to hear still sob and sigh.
At dawn again I go my way
And only bid my host goodbye.

Xiaoyi Cheating Wang Xizhi's Calligraphic Work (Titled Preface to the Poems Composed at the Orchid Pavilion, partial), Tang Dynasty, Yan Liben

杜 甫 Du Fu

月夜忆舍弟

戍鼓断人行，边秋一雁声。
露从今夜白，月是故乡明。
有弟皆分散，无家问死生。
寄书长不达，况乃未休兵。

THINKING OF MY BROTHER ON A MOONLIT NIGHT

War drums break people's journey drear;
A swan honks on autumn frontier.
Dew turns into frost since tonight;
The moon viewed at home is more bright.
I've brothers scattered here and there;
For our life or death none would care.
Letters can't reach where I intend;
Alas! the war's not come to an end.

帝伯宗在位二年

历代帝王图（局部）唐代 阎立本
Emperors of the Past Dynasties (partial), Tang Dynasty, Yan Liben

杜 甫 Du Fu

蜀相

蜀相祠堂何处寻？锦官城外柏森森。
映阶碧草自春色，隔叶黄鹂空好音。
三顾频烦天下计，两朝开济老臣心。
出师未捷身先死，长使英雄泪满襟。

TEMPLE OF THE PREMIER OF SHU

Where is the famous premier's temple to be found?
Outside the Town of Brocade with cypresses around.
In vain before the steps spring grass grows green and long,
And amid the leaves golden orioles sing their song.
Thrice the king visited him for the State's gains and pains;
He served heart and soul the kingdom during two reigns.
But he died before he accomplished his career.
How could heroes not wet their sleeves with tear on tear!

萧翼赚兰亭图（局部） 唐代 阎立本
Xiaoyi Cheating Wang Xizhi's Calligraphic Work (Titled Preface to the Poems Composed at the Orchid Pavilion, partial), Tang Dynasty, Yan Liben

杜 甫 Du Fu

客至

舍南舍北皆春水，但见群鸥日日来。
花径不曾缘客扫，蓬门今始为君开。
盘飧市远无兼味，樽酒家贫只旧醅。
肯与邻翁相对饮，隔篱呼取尽余杯。

FOR A GUEST

North and south of my cottage winds spring water green;
I see but flocks of gulls coming from day to day.
The footpath strewn with fallen blooms is not swept clean;
My wicket gate is opened but for you today.
Far from market, I can afford but simple dish;
Being not rich, I've only old wine for our cup.
To drink together with my neighbor if you wish,
I'll call him o'er the fence to finish the wine up.

虢国夫人游春图（局部） 唐代 张萱
Lady of Guo State's Spring Outing (partial), Tang Dynasty, Zhang Xuan

杜 甫 Du Fu

春夜喜雨

好雨知时节，当春乃发生。
随风潜入夜，润物细无声。
野径云俱黑，江船火独明。
晓看红湿处，花重锦官城。

HAPPY RAIN ON A SPRING NIGHT

Good rain knows its time right;
It will fall when comes spring.
With wind it steals in night;
Mute, it moistens each thing.
O'er wild lanes dark cloud spreads;
In boat a lantern looms.
Dawn sees saturated reds;
The town's heavy with blooms.

人物故事图册（局部） 唐代 阎立本（传）
Album of Figures and Stories (partial), Tang Dynasty, Yan Liben (purported)

杜 甫 Du Fu

茅屋为秋风所破歌

八月秋高风怒号，卷我屋上三重茅。
茅飞渡江洒江郊，高者挂罥长林梢，下者飘转沉塘坳。
南村群童欺我老无力，忍能对面为盗贼。公然抱茅入竹去。
唇焦口燥呼不得，归来倚杖自叹息。
俄顷风定云墨色，秋天漠漠向昏黑。
布衾多年冷似铁，骄儿恶卧踏里裂。
床头屋漏无干处，雨脚如麻未断绝。
自经丧乱少睡眠，长夜沾湿何由彻！
安得广厦千万间，大庇天下寒士俱欢颜，风雨不动安如山！
呜呼！何时眼前突兀见此屋，吾庐独破受冻死亦足！

MY COTTACE UNROOFED BY AUTUMN GALES

In the eighth moon the autumn gales furiously howl;
They roll up three layers of straw from my thatched bower.
The straw flies across the river and spreads in shower,
Some hanging knotted on the tops of trees that tower,
Some swirling down and sinking into water foul.

Urchins from southern village know Im old and weak;
They rob me to my face without a blush on the cheek,
And holding armfuls of straw, into bamboos they sneak.
In vain I call them till my lips are parched and dry;
Again alone, I lean on my cane and sigh.
Shortly the gale subsides and clouds turn dark as ink;
The autumn skies are shrouded and in darkness sink.
My cotton quilt is cold, for years it has been worn;
My restless children kick in sleep and it is torn.

十六神骏图（局部） 唐代 韩干
16 Horses with Various Poses (partial), Tang Dynasty, Han Gan

The roof leaks o'er beds, leaving no corner dry;
Without cease the rain falls thick and fast from the sky.
After the troubled times troubled has been my sleep.
Wet through, how can I pass the night so long, so deep!
Could I get mansions covering ten thousand miles,
I'd house all scholars poor and make them beam with smiles.
In wind and rain these mansions would stand like mountains high.
Alas! should these houses appear before my eye,
Frozen in my unroofed cot, content I'd die.

游骑图（局部） 唐代 佚名
A Man Traveling around on Horseback (partial), Tang Dynasty, Anonymous

杜 甫 Du Fu

闻官军收河南河北

剑外忽传收蓟北，初闻涕泪满衣裳。
却看妻子愁何在，漫卷诗书喜欲狂。
白首放歌须纵酒，青春作伴好还乡。
即从巴峡穿巫峡，便下襄阳向洛阳。

RECAPTURE OF THE REGIONS NORTH AND SOUTH OF THE YELLOW RIVER

'Tis said the Northern Gate is recaptured of late;
When the news reach my ears, my gown is wet with tears.
Staring at my wife's face, of grief I find no trace;
Rolling up my verse books, my joy like madness looks.
Though I am white-haired, still I'd sing and drink my fill.
With verdure spring's aglow, 'tis time we homeward go.
We shall sail all the way through Three Gorges in a day.
Going down to Xiangyang, we'll come up to Luoyang.

辋川图 唐代 王维
Mountain Wangchuan, Tang Dynasty, Wang Wei

杜 甫 Du Fu

绝句

两个黄鹂鸣翠柳,
一行白鹭上青天。
窗含西岭千秋雪,
门泊东吴万里船。

A QUATRAIN

Two golden orioles sing amid the willows green;
A flock of white egrets flies into the blue sky.
My window frames the snow-crowned western mountain scene;
My door oft says to eastward-going ships "Goodbye!"

杜 甫　Du Fu

旅夜书怀

细草微风岸，危樯独夜舟。
星垂平野阔，月涌大江流。
名岂文章著？官应老病休。
飘飘何所似？天地一沙鸥。

呈马图卷（局部） 唐代 韩干
Horses Presented to Court (partial),
Tang Dynasty, Han Gan

Mooring at Night

Riverside grass caressed by wind so light,
A lonely mast seems to pierce lonely night.
The boundless plain fringed with stars hanging low,
The moon surges with the river on the flow.
Will fame ever come to a man of letters
Old, ill, retired, no official life betters?
What do I look like, drifting on so free?
A wild gull seeking shelter on the sea.

杜 甫 Du Fu

登岳阳楼

昔闻洞庭水,今上岳阳楼。
吴楚东南坼,乾坤日夜浮。
亲朋无一字,老病有孤舟。
戎马关山北,凭轩涕泗流。

九成避暑图（局部） 唐代 李思训
Imperial Summer Palace (partial), Tang Dynasty, Li Sixun

ON YUEYANG TOWER

Long have I heard of Dongting Lake;
Now I'm on Yueyang Tower's height.
Here Eastern and Southern States break;
Here sun and moon float day and night.
No word comes from kinsfolk and friends;
A boat bears my declining years.
War is raging on the northern ends.
O what can I do but shed tears!

宫乐图（局部） 唐代 佚名
Palace Maidens Playing Instruments (partial), Tang Dynasty, Anonymous

岑 参 Cen Shen

白雪歌送武判官归京

北风卷地白草折，胡天八月即飞雪。
忽如一夜春风来，千树万树梨花开。
散入珠帘湿罗幕，狐裘不暖锦衾薄。
将军角弓不得控，都护铁衣冷难着。
瀚海阑干百丈冰，愁云惨淡万里凝。
中军置酒饮归客，胡琴琵琶与羌笛。
纷纷暮雪下辕门，风掣红旗冻不翻。
轮台东门送君去，去时雪满天山路。
山回路转不见君，雪上空留马行处。

Cen Shen (715?–770) and Gao Shi were renowned frontier fortress poets, and their poem styles were similar. Cen's works feature frontier landscape, wars, culture and customs, with romantic style, magnificent momentum and creativity contents. In the golden age of the Tang Dynasty, he was an accomplished poet, with the largest production of frontier poetry.

演乐图（局部） 唐代 周昉（传）
Music Performance (partial), Tang Dynasty, Zhou Fang (purported)

Song of White Snow in Farewell to Secretary Wu Going Back to the Capital

Snapping the pallid grass, the northern wind whirls low;
In the eighth moon the Tartar sky is filled with snow
As if the vernal breeze had come back overnight,
Adorning thousands of pear trees with blossoms white.
Flakes enter pearled blinds and wet the silken screen;
No furs of fox can warm us nor brocade quilts green.
The general cannot draw his rigid bow with ease;
E'en the commissioner in coat of mail would freeze.
A thousand feet o'er cracked wilderness ice piles,
And gloomy clouds hang sad and drear for miles and miles.
We drink in headquarters to our guest homeward bound;
With Tartar lutes, pipas and pipes the camps resound.
Snow in large flakes at dusk falls heavy on camp gate;
The frozen red flag in the wind won't undulate.
At eastern gate of Wheel Tower we bid goodbye
On the snow-covered road to Heaven's Mountain high.
I watch his horse go past a bend and, lost to sight,
His track will soon be buried up by snow in flight.

神骏图卷（局部） 唐代 韩干
Monk Zhidun Watching Horse (partial), Tang Dynasty, Han Gan

岑 参 Cen Shen

逢入京使

故园东望路漫漫，
双袖龙钟泪不干。
马上相逢无纸笔，
凭君传语报平安。

ON MEETING A MESSENGER GOING TO THE CAPITAL

I look eastward, long, long my homeward road appears.
My old arms tremble and my sleeves are wet with tears.
Meeting you on horseback, with what brush can I write?
I can but ask you to tell them I am all right.

神骏图卷（局部）
Monk Zhidun Watching Horse (partial)

张 继 Zhang Ji

枫桥夜泊

月落乌啼霜满天，
江枫渔火对愁眠。
姑苏城外寒山寺，
夜半钟声到客船。

Mooring by Maple Bridge at Night

At moonset cry the crows, streaking the frosty sky;
Dimly lit fishing boats 'neath maples sadly lie.

仙山楼观图卷（局部） 唐代 李昭道（传）
Fairy Mountains and Buildings (partial), Tang Dynasty, Li Zhaodao (purported)

    Beyond the city wall, from Temple of Cold Hill
    Bells break the ship-borne roamer's dream and midnight still.

Zhang Ji's works were mostly created during his travel, using clear and vigorous style. Instead of squeamish refinement of words, he only used simple words and a metaphor skill to both describe landscape and convey some sentiments and philosophies. His *Zhang Cibu Poetry Anthology* has been preserved over the times. Among his less than existing 50 poems, *Mooning By Maple Bridge at Night* is the most popular.

人物故事图册（局部） 唐代 阎立本（传）
Album of Figures and Stories (partial), Tang Dynasty, Yan Liben (purported)

韦应物　Wei Yingwu

滁州西涧

独怜幽草涧边生，
上有黄鹂深树鸣。
春潮带雨晚来急，
野渡无人舟自横。

ON THE WEST STREAM AT CHUZHOU

Alone, I like the riverside where green grass grows
And golden orioles sing amid the leafy trees.
When showers fall at dusk, the river overflows;
A lonely boat athwart the ferry floats at ease.

Wei Yingwu (737–792?) was a celebrated landscape poet in the Tang Dynasty. His poems with simple words feature sceneries to reflect his clam and peace life in seclusion. He wrote *Wei Suzhou Anthology*.

Court Ladies Preparing Newly-Woven Silk (partial), Tang Dynasty, Zhang Xuan

孟 郊 Meng Jiao

游子吟

慈母手中线，游子身上衣。

临行密密缝，意恐迟迟归。

谁言寸草心，报得三春晖？

SONG OF THE PARTING SON

From the threads a mother's hand weaves

A gown for parting son is made,

Sewn stitch by stitch before he leaves

For fear his return be delayed,

Such kindness as young grass receives

From the warm sun can be repaid?

Meng Jiao (751–814) completed Jinshi level of imperial examination at the age of 46 years after two fails, but realized his political ambition couldn't be fulfilled in official career and so he neglected his government affairs to engage in enjoying natural sceneries and writing poems. He often employed themes of poverty and cold in his poems to express his inner sufferings. Together with Jia Dao, he was renowned for the forcefulness and harshness of their poems. He left *Meng Dongye Anthology*.

捣练图（局部）
Court Ladies Preparing Newly-Woven Silk (partial)

Emperor's Journey to Shu (partial), Tang Dynasty, Li Zhaodao

韩 愈 Han Yu

早春呈水部张十八员外

天街小雨润如酥，

草色遥看近却无。

最是一年春好处，

绝胜烟柳满皇都。

EARLY SPRING WRITTEN FOR SECRETARY ZHANG JI

The royal streets are moistened by a creamlike rain;
Green grass can be perceived afar but not near by.
It's the best time of a year that spring tries in vain
With the capital veiled in willows to outvie.

Han Yu (768–824) was a writer, thinker, philosopher and politician. He led a revolt against classical style of writing, a formal, richly ornamented literary style, and was ranked the first among the "Eight Great Prose Masters of the Tang and Song Dynasties". Meanwhile, Along with Liu Zongyuan, he was a founder of the Classical Prose Movement. His poems were noted for novelty and became influential among the Song Dynasty writers and poets. The *Mr. Changli Anthology* was left by him.

张 籍 Zhang Ji

节妇吟

君知妾有夫,赠妾双明珠。
感君缠绵意,系在红罗襦。
妾家高楼连苑起,良人执戟明光里。
知君用心如日月,事夫誓拟同生死。
还君明珠双泪垂,恨不相逢未嫁时。

Zhang Ji (766?–830?) was the initiator and supporter of New *Yuefu* Movement which took place in the middle-age Tang Dynasty, designed to revive the poems in *Yuefu* style. He was the first student of Han Yu. Together with Wang Jianqi, he was known for their poems in *Yuefu* style. His works were created to mainly reflect the social reality by contrast methods. Meanwhile, he excelled in describing various real figures in detail in his poems, and as a result made great achievements in art. He completed *Zhang Siye Anthology*.

挥扇仕女图（局部） 唐代 周昉

Court Ladies and Their Servants (partial), Tang Dynasty, Zhou Fang

REPLY OF A CHASTE WIFE

You know I love my husband best,
Yet you send me two bright pearls still.
I hang them within my red silk vest,
So grateful I'm for your good will.
You see my house o'erlooks the garden and
My husband guards the palace, halberd in hand.
I know your heart as noble as the sun in the skies,
But I have sworn to serve my husband all my life.
With your twin pearls I send back two tears from my eyes.
Why did we not meet before I was made a wife?

韩熙载夜宴图（局部） 唐代 顾闳中
Banquet Scene in Han Xizai's Mansion (partial), Tang Dynasty, Gu Hongzhong

刘禹锡　Liu Yuxi

酬乐天扬州初逢席上见赠

巴山楚水凄凉地，二十三年弃置身。
怀旧空吟闻笛赋，到乡翻似烂柯人。
沉舟侧畔千帆过，病树前头万木春。
今日听君歌一曲，暂凭杯酒长精神。

Reply to Bai Juyi Whom I Meet for the First Time at a Banquet in Yangzhou

O western mountains and southern streams desolate,
Where I, an exile, lived for twenty years and three!
To mourn for my departed friends I come too late;
In my native land I look like human debris.
Hundreds of sails pass by the side of sunken ship;
Thousands of flowers bloom ahead of injured tree.
Today I hear you chant the praise of comradeship;
I wish this cup of wine might well inspirit me.

Liu Yuxi (772–842) was a writer, philosopher and official in the Tang Dynasty, also known for the bold and uninhibited style of his poems. He also excelled in writing folk-style poems including *Song of Bamboo Branch*, *Song of Willow Branch* and *Song of Field-planting*, which is a new style in Tang poetry. His philosophical writing titled *Tianlun* (*On the Relationship between Heaven and Man*) including three parts, expounds on the materiality of heaven and the origin of heaven-man relationship on the basis of the opinion of the materialism. The *Liu Mengde Anthology* is one of his works.

韩熙载夜宴图（局部）
Banquet Scene in Han Xizai's Mansion (partial)

簪花仕女图（局部） 唐代 周昉
Court Ladies Wearing Flowered Headdresses (partial), Tang Dynasty, Zhou Fang

刘禹锡　Liu Yuxi

乌衣巷

朱雀桥边野草花，
乌衣巷口夕阳斜。
旧时王谢堂前燕，
飞入寻常百姓家。

THE STREET OF MANSIONS

Beside the Bridge of Birds rank grasses overgrow;
O'er the Street of Mansions the setting sun hangs low.
Swallows that skimmed by painted eaves in bygone days
Are dipping now among the humble homes' doorways.

白居易　Bai Juyi

卖炭翁

卖炭翁，伐薪烧炭南山中。

满面尘灰烟火色，两鬓苍苍十指黑。

卖炭得钱何所营？身上衣裳口中食。

Bai Juyi (772–846) was a government official and romantic poet in the Tang Dynasty. In addition to various themes and styles, his poems were accessible even to the old women. He wrote *Mr. Bai Anthology*. His masterpieces include *The Everlasting Regret*, *The Old Charcoal Seller* and *Song of A Pipa Player*.

五牛图（局部） 唐代 韩滉
Five Cows with Different Poses (partial), Tang Dynasty, Han Huang

可怜身上衣正单，心忧炭贱愿天寒。
夜来城外一尺雪，晓驾炭车辗冰辙。
牛困人饥日已高，市南门外泥中歇。
翩翩两骑来是谁？黄衣使者白衫儿。
手把文书口称敕，回车叱牛牵向北。
一车炭，千余斤，宫使驱将惜不得。
半匹红绡一丈绫，系向牛头充炭直。

孔子弟子像卷（局部） 唐代 阎立本
Portraits of Disciples of Confucius (partial), Tang Dynasty, Yan Liben

THE OLD CHARCOAL SELLER

What does the old man fare?
He cuts the wood in southern hill and fires his ware,
His face is grimed with smoke and streaked with ash and dust,
His temples grizzled and his fingers all turned black.
The money earned by selling charcoal is not just
Enough for food for his mouth and clothing for his back.
Though his coat is thin, he hopes winter will set in,
For cold weather will keep up the charcoal's good price.
At night a foot of snow falls outside city walls;
At dawn his charcoal cart crushes ruts in the ice.
The sun is high, the ox tired out and hungry he;
Outside the southern gate in snow and slush they rest.
Two riders canter up, Alas! who can they be?
Two palace heralds in the yellow jackets dressed.
Decree in hand, which is imperial order, one says;
They turn the cart about and at the ox they shout.
A cartload of charcoal a thousand catties weighs;
They drive the cart away. What dare the old man say?
Ten feet of silk and twenty feet of gauze deep red—
That is the payment they fasten to the ox's head.

白居易　Bai Juyi

长恨歌

汉皇重色思倾国，御宇多年求不得。
杨家有女初长成，养在深闺人未识。
天生丽质难自弃，一朝选在君王侧。
回眸一笑百媚生，六宫粉黛无颜色。
春寒赐浴华清池，温泉水滑洗凝脂。
侍儿扶起娇无力，始是新承恩泽时。
云鬓花颜金步摇，芙蓉帐暖度春宵。
春宵苦短日高起，从此君王不早朝。

承欢侍宴无闲暇，春从春游夜专夜。
后宫佳丽三千人，三千宠爱在一身。
金屋妆成娇侍夜，玉楼宴罢醉和春。
姊妹弟兄皆列土，可怜光彩生门户。

簪花仕女图 唐代 周昉
Court Ladies Wearing Flowered Headdresses, Tang Dynasty, Zhou Fang

遂令天下父母心，不重生男重生女。
骊宫高处入青云，仙乐风飘处处闻。
缓歌慢舞凝丝竹，尽日君王看不足。
渔阳鼙鼓动地来，惊破霓裳羽衣曲。

九重城阙烟尘生，千乘万骑西南行。
翠华摇摇行复止，西出都门百余里。
六军不发无奈何，宛转蛾眉马前死。
花钿委地无人收，翠翘金雀玉搔头。
君王掩面救不得，回看血泪相和流。
黄埃散漫风萧索，云栈萦纡登剑阁。
峨嵋山下少人行，旌旗无光日色薄。
蜀江水碧蜀山青，圣主朝朝暮暮情。

簪花仕女图（局部）
Court Ladies Wearing Flowered Headdresses (partial)

行宫见月伤心色，夜雨闻铃肠断声。
天旋地转回龙驭，到此踌躇不能去。
马嵬坡下泥土中，不见玉颜空死处。
君臣相顾尽沾衣，东望都门信马归。
归来池苑皆依旧，太液芙蓉未央柳。
芙蓉如面柳如眉，对此如何不泪垂。
春风桃李花开日，秋雨梧桐叶落时。
西宫南内多秋草，落叶满阶红不扫。

梨园弟子白发新，椒房阿监青娥老。
夕殿萤飞思悄然，孤灯挑尽未成眠。
迟迟钟鼓初长夜，耿耿星河欲曙天。
鸳鸯瓦冷霜华重，翡翠衾寒谁与共？
悠悠生死别经年，魂魄不曾来入梦。
临邛道士鸿都客，能以精诚致魂魄。
为感君王展转思，遂教方士殷勤觅。
排空驭气奔如电，升天入地求之遍。

上穷碧落下黄泉，两处茫茫皆不见。
忽闻海上有仙山，山在虚无缥缈间。
楼阁玲珑五云起，其中绰约多仙子。
中有一人字太真，雪肤花貌参差是。
金阙西厢叩玉扃，转教小玉报双成。
闻道汉家天子使，九华帐里梦魂惊。
揽衣推枕起徘徊，珠箔银屏迤逦开。
云鬓半偏新睡觉，花冠不整下堂来。

簪花仕女图（局部）
Court Ladies Wearing Flowered Headdresses (partial)

风吹仙袂飘飘举，犹似霓裳羽衣舞。
玉容寂寞泪阑干，梨花一枝春带雨。
含情凝睇谢君王，一别音容两渺茫。
昭阳殿里恩爱绝，蓬莱宫中日月长。
回头下望人寰处，不见长安见尘雾。
唯将旧物表深情，钿合金钗寄将去。
钗留一股合一扇，钗擘黄金合分钿。
但教心似金钿坚，天上人间会相见。

临别殷勤重寄词，词中有誓两心知。
七月七日长生殿，夜半无人私语时。
在天愿作比翼鸟，在地愿为连理枝。
天长地久有时尽，此恨绵绵无绝期。

THE EVERLASTING REGRET

The beauty-loving monarch longed year after year
To find a beautiful lady without a peer.
A maiden of the Yangs to womanhood just grown,
In inner chambers bred, to the world was unknown.
Endowed with natural beauty too hard to hide,
She was chosen one day to be the monarch's bride.
Turning her head, she smiled so sweet and full of grace
That she outshone in six palaces the fairest face.
She bathed in glassy water of warm-fountain Pool,
Which laved and smoothed her creamy skin when spring was cool.
Without her maids' support, she was too tired to move,
And this was when she first received the monarch's love.

Flower-like face and cloud-like hair, golden-headdressed,
In lotus-adorned curtain she spent the night blessed.
She slept till the sun rose high for the blessed night was short,
From then on the monarch held no longer morning court.

In revels as in feasts she shared her lord's delight,
His companion on trips and his mistress at night.
In inner palace dwelt three thousand ladies fair;
On her alone was lavished royal love and care.
Her beauty served the night when dressed up in Golden Bower;
She was drunk with wine and spring at banquet in Jade Tower.
Her sisters and brothers all received rank and fief
And honors showered on her household, to the grief
Of fathers and mothers who would rather give birth
To a fair maiden than to any son on earth.
The lofty palace towered high into the cloud;
With divine music borne on the breeze, the air was loud.
Seeing slow dance and hearing fluted or stringed song,
The emperor was never tired the whole day long.
But rebels beat their war drums, making the earth quake
And "Song of Rainbow Skirt and Coat of Feathers" break.

A cloud of dust was raised o'er city walls nine-fold;
Thousands of chariots and horsemen southwestward rolled.
Imperial flags moved slowly now and halted then,
And thirty miles from Western Gate they stopped again.
Six armies — what could be done? — would not march with speed
Unless fair Lady Yang be killed before the steed.
None would pick up her hairpin fallen on the ground
Nor golden bird nor comb with which her head was crowned.
The monarch could not save her and hid his face in fear;

簪花仕女图（局部）
Court Ladies Wearing Flowered Headdresses (partial)

韩熙载夜宴图（局部） 唐代 顾闳中
Banquet Scene in Han Xizai's Mansion (partial), Tang Dynasty, Gu Hongzhong

Turning his head, he saw her blood mix with his tear.
The yellow dust widespread, the wind blew desolate;
A serpentine plank path led to cloud-capped Sword Gate.
Below the Eyebrows Mountains wayfarers were few;
In fading sunlight royal standards lost their hue.
On Western water blue and Western mountains green
The monarch's heart was daily gnawed by sorrow keen.

The moon viewed from his tent shed a soul-searing light;
The bells heard in night rain made a heart-rending sound.
Suddenly turned the tide. Returning from his flight,
The monarch could not tear himself away from the ground
Where 'mid the clods beneath the Slope he couldn't forget
The fair-faced Lady Yang who was unfairly slain.
He looked at his courtiers, with tears his robe was wet;
They rode east to the capital but with loose rein.
Come back, he found her pond and garden in old place,
With lotus in the lake and willows by the hall.
Willow leaves like her brows and lotus like her face,
At the sight of all these, how could his tears not fall.
Or when in vernal breeze were peach and plum full-blown
Or when in autumn rain parasol leaves were shed?
In Western as in Southern Court was grass o'ergrown;
With fallen leaves unswept the marble steps turned red.

韩熙载夜宴图 （局部）
Banquet Scene in Han Xizai's Mansion (partial)

Actors, although still young, began to have hair grey;
Eunuchs and waiting maids looked old in palace deep.
Fireflies flitting the hall, mutely he pined away;
The lonely lampwick burned out, still he could not sleep.
Slowly beat drums and rang bells, night began to grow long;
Bright shone the Starry Stream, daybreak seemed to come late.
The love-bird tiles grew chilly with hoar frost so strong;
His kingfisher quilt was cold, not shared by a mate.
One long, long year the dead with the living was parted;
Her soul came not in dreams to see the broken-hearted,
A taoist sorcerer came to the palace door,
Skilled to summon the spirits from the other shore.
Moved by the monarch's yearning for the departed fair,
He was ordered to seek for her everywhere.
Borne on the air, like flash of lightning he flew;
In heaven and on earth he searched through and through.

Up to the azure vault and down to deepest place,
Nor above nor below could he e'er find her trace.
He learned that on the sea were fairy mountains proud
Which now appeared now disappeared amid the cloud
Of rainbow colors, where rose magnificent bowers
And dwelt so many fairies as graceful as flowers.
Among them was a queen whose name was Ever True;
Her snow-white skin and sweet face might afford a clue.

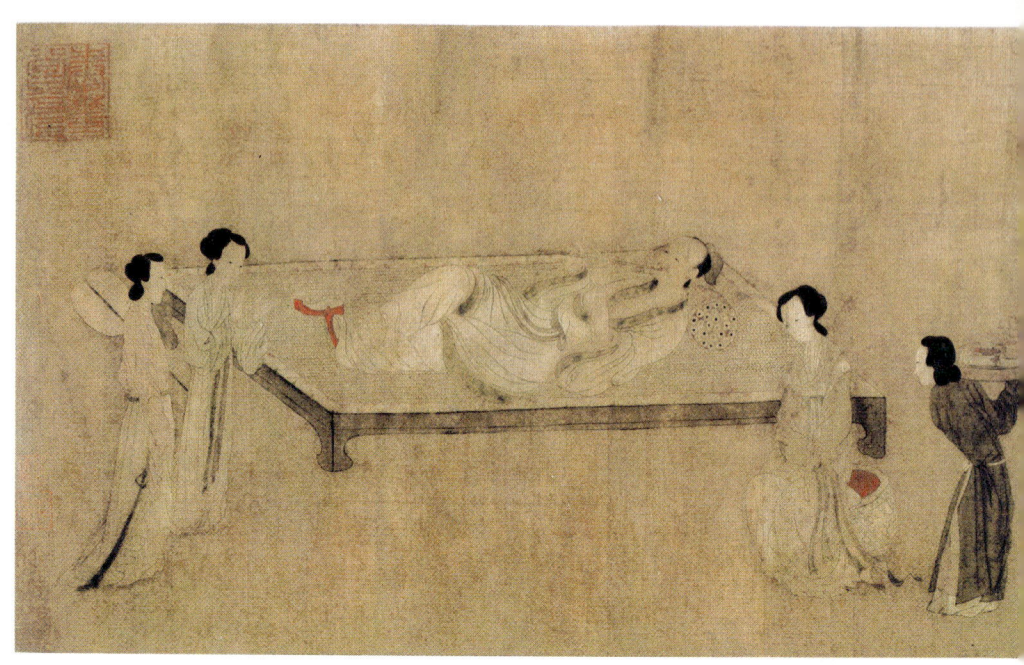

Knocking at western gate of palace hall, he bade
The fair porter to inform the queen's waiting maid.
When she heard that there came the monarch's embassy,
The queen was startled out of dreams in her canopy.
Pushing aside the pillow, she rose and got dressed,
Passing through silver screen and pearl shade to meet the guest.
Her cloud-like hair awry, not full awake at all,
Her flowery cap slanted, she came into the hall.

The wind blew up her fairy sleeves and made them float
As if she danced still "Rainbow Skirt and Feathered Coat."
Her jade-white face crisscrossed with tears in lonely world
Like a spray of pear blossoms in spring rain impearled.
She bade him thank her lord, lovesick and broken-hearted;

明皇合乐图 唐代 张萱
Symphony of Emperor Xuanzong and Court Ladies, Tang Dynasty, Zhang Xuan

They knew nothing of each other after they parted.
Love and happiness long ended within palace walls;
Days and nights appeared long in the Fairyland halls.
Turning her head and fixing on the earth her gaze,
She found no capital 'mid clouds of dust and haze.
To show her love was deep, she took out keepsakes old
For him to carry back, hairpin and case of gold.
Keeping one side of the case and one wing of the pin,
She sent to her lord the other half of the twin.
"If our two hearts as firm as the gold should remain,
In heaven or on earth some time we'll meet again."

At parting, she confided to the messenger
A secret vow known only to her lord and her.
On seventh day of seventh moon when none was near,
At midnight in Long Long-life Hall he whispered in her ear:
"On high, we'd be two birds flying wing to wing;
On earth, two trees with branches twined from spring to spring."
The boundless sky and endless earth may pass away,
But this vow unfulfilled will be regretted for aye.

宫乐图（局部）　唐代　佚名
Palace Maidens Playing Instrument (partial), Tang Dynasty, Anonymous

白居易　Bai Juyi

琵琶行

浔阳江头夜送客，枫叶荻花秋瑟瑟。
主人下马客在船，举酒欲饮无管弦。
醉不成欢惨将别，别时茫茫江浸月。
忽闻水上琵琶声，主人忘归客不发。
寻声暗问弹者谁，琵琶声停欲语迟。
移船相近邀相见，添酒回灯重开宴。
千呼万唤始出来，犹抱琵琶半遮面。
转轴拨弦三两声，未成曲调先有情。
弦弦掩抑声声思，似诉平生不得志。
低眉信手续续弹，说尽心中无限事。

轻拢慢捻抹复挑，初为《霓裳》后《六幺》。
大弦嘈嘈如急雨，小弦切切如私语。
嘈嘈切切错杂弹，大珠小珠落玉盘。
间关莺语花底滑，幽咽泉流冰下难。

宫乐图（局部）
Palace Maidens Playing Instrument (partial)

冰泉冷涩弦凝绝，凝绝不通声渐歇。
别有幽愁暗恨生，此时无声胜有声。
银瓶乍破水浆迸，铁骑突出刀枪鸣。
曲终收拨当心画，四弦一声如裂帛。
东船西舫悄无言，唯见江心秋月白。
沉吟放拨插弦中，整顿衣裳起敛容。
自言本是京城女，家在虾蟆陵下住。
十三学得琵琶成，名属教坊第一部。

曲罢曾教善才伏，妆成每被秋娘妒。
五陵年少争缠头，一曲红绡不知数。
钿头云篦击节碎，血色罗裙翻酒污。
今年欢笑复明年，秋月春风等闲度。
弟走从军阿姨死，暮去朝来颜色故。
门前冷落车马稀，老大嫁作商人妇。
商人重利轻别离，前月浮梁买茶去。
去来江口守空船，绕船月明江水寒。
夜深忽梦少年事，梦啼妆泪红阑干。
我闻琵琶已叹息，又闻此语重唧唧。
同是天涯沦落人，相逢何必曾相识！
我从去年辞帝京，谪居卧病浔阳城。

宫乐图（局部）
Palace Maidens Playing Instrument (partial)

宫乐图（局部）
Palace Maidens Playing Instrument (partial)

浔阳地僻无音乐，终岁不闻丝竹声。
住近湓江地低湿，黄芦苦竹绕宅生。
其间旦暮闻何物？杜鹃啼血猿哀鸣。
春江花朝秋月夜，往往取酒还独倾。
岂无山歌与村笛，呕哑嘲哳难为听。
今夜闻君琵琶语，如听仙乐耳暂明。
莫辞更坐弹一曲，为君翻作琵琶行。
感我此言良久立，却坐促弦弦转急。
凄凄不似向前声，满座重闻皆掩泣。
座中泣下谁最多？江州司马青衫湿。

SONG OF A PIPA PLAYER

One night by riverside I bade a friend goodbye;
In maple leaves and rushes autumn seemed to sigh.
My friend and I dismounted and came into the boat;
We wished to drink but there was no music afloat.
Without flute songs we drank cur cups with heavy heart;
The moonbeams blent with water when we were to part.
Suddenly o'er the stream we heard a pipa sound;
I forgot to go home and the guest stood spell-bound.

韩熙载夜宴图（局部） 唐代 顾闳中
Banquet Scene in Han Xizai's Mansion (partial), Tang Dynasty, Gu Hongzhong

We followed where the music led to find the player,
But heard the pipa stop and no music in the air.
We moved our boat towards the one whence came the strain,
Brought back the lamp, asked for more wine and drank again.
Repeatedly we called for the fair player till
She came, her face half hidden behind a pipa still.
She turned the pegs and tested twice or thrice each string;
Before a tune was played we heard her feelings sing.
Each string she plucked, each note she struck with pathos strong,
All seemed to say she'd missed her dreams all her life long.
Head bent, she played with unpremeditated art
On and on to pour out her overflowing heart.

She lightly plucked, slowly stroked and twanged loud
The song of "Green Waist" after that of "Rainbow Cloud."
The thick strings loudly thrummed like the pettering rain;
The fine strings softly tinkled in a murmuring strain.
When mingling loud and soft notes were together played,
You heard large and small pearls cascade on plate of jade.
Now you heard orioles warble in flowery land,
Then a sobbing stream run along a beach of sand.
But the stream seemed so cold as to tighten the string;
From tightenied strings no more sound could be heard to sing.
Still we heard hidden grief and vague regret concealed;
Then music expressed far less than silence revealed.
Suddenly we heard water burst a silver jar,
And the clash of spears and sabres come from afar.

伎乐图（局部） 唐代壁画 佚名
Ladies Playing Instrument (partial), Mural of the Tang Dynasty, Anonymous

She made a central sweep when the music was ending;
The four strings made one sound, as of silk one was rending.
Silence reigned left and right of the boat, east and west;
We saw but autumn moon white in the river's breast.
She slid the plectrum pensively between the strings,
Smoothed out her dress and rose with a composed mien.
"I spent," she said, "in the capital my early springs,
Where at the foot of Mount of Toads my home had been.
At thirteen I learned on the pipa how to play,
And my name was among the primas of the day.

I won my master's admiration for my skill
My beauty was envied by songstresses fair still.
The gallant young men vied to shower gifts on me;
One tune played, countless silk rolls were given with glee.
Beating time, I let silver comb and pin drop down,
And spilt-out wine oft stained my blood-red silken gown.
From year to year I laughed my joyous life away
On moonlit autumn night as windy vernal day.
My younger brother left for war, and died my maid;
Days passed, nights came, and my beauty began to fade.
Fewer and fewer were cabs and steeds at my door;
I married a smug merchant when my prime was o'er.
The merchant cared for money much more than for me;
One month ago he went away to purchase tea,
Leaving his lonely wife alone in empty boat;
Shrouded in moonlight, on the cold river I float.
Deep in the night I dreamed of happy bygone years,

乐舞图 唐墓壁画 佚名
Nstrument Playing, Mural in the Tang Tomb, Anonymous

And woke to find my rouged face crisscrossed with tears."
Listening to her sad music, I sighed with pain;
Hearing her story, I sighed again and again.
"Both of us in misfortune go from shore to shore.
Meeting now, need we have known each other before?
I was banished from the capital last year
To live degraded and ill in this city here.

树下仕女屏风图 唐墓壁画 佚名
A Beauty under the Tree, Mural in the Tang Tomb, Anonymous

The city's too remote to know melodious song,
So I have never heard music all the year long.
I dwell by riverbank on a low and damp ground
In a house with wild reeds and stunted bamboos around.
What is here to be heard from daybreak till nightfall
But gibbon's cry and cuckoo's homeward-going call?
By blooming riverside and under autumn moon
I've often taken wine up and drunk it alone.
Though I have mountain songs and village pipes to hear,
Yet they are crude and strident and grate on the ear.
Listening to you playing on pipa tonight,
With your music divine e'en my hearing seems bright.
Will you sit down and play for us a tune once more?
I'll write for you an ode to the pipa I adore."
Touched by what I said, the player stood for long,
Then sat down, tore at strings and played another song.
So sad, so drear, so different, it moved us deep;
Those who heard it hid the face and began to weep.
Of all the company at table who wept most?
It was none other than the exiled blue-robed host.

十六神骏图（局部） 唐代 韩干
16 Horses with Various Poses (partial), Tang Dynasty, Han Gan

白居易　Bai Juyi

赋得古原草送别

离离原上草，一岁一枯荣。
野火烧不尽，春风吹又生。
远芳侵古道，晴翠接荒城。
又送王孙去，萋萋满别情。

GRASS ON THE ANCIENT PLAIN — FAREWELL TO A FRIEND

Wild grasses spread o'er ancient plain;
With spring and fall they come and go.
Fire tries to burn them up in vain;
They rise again when spring winds blow.
Their fragrance overruns the way;
Their green invades the ruined town.
To see my friend going away,
My sorrow grows like grass o'ergrown.

虢国夫人游春图（局部）唐代 张萱
Lady of Guo State's Spring Outing (partial), Tang Dynasty, Zhang Xuan

白居易　Bai Juyi

钱塘湖春行

孤山寺北贾亭西，水面初平云脚低。
几处早莺争暖树，谁家新燕啄春泥。
乱花渐欲迷人眼，浅草才能没马蹄。
最爱湖东行不足，绿杨阴里白沙堤。

ON LAKE QIANTANG IN SPRING

West of Pavilion Jia and north of Lonely Hill,
Water brims level with the bank and clouds hang low.
Disputing for sunny trees, early orioles trill;
Pecking vernal mud in, young swallows come and go.
A riot of blooms begin to dazzle the eye;
Amid short grass the horse hoofs can barely be seen.
I love best the east of the lake under the sky:
The bank paved with white sand is shaded by willows green.

虢国夫人游春图（局部） 唐代 张萱
Lady of Guo State's Spring Outing (partial), Tang Dynasty, Zhang Xuan

柳宗元 Liu Zongyuan

江雪

千山鸟飞绝，

万径人踪灭。

孤舟蓑笠翁，

独钓寒江雪。

Fishing in Snow

From hill to hill no bird in flight;

From path to path no man in sight.

A lonely fisherman afloat

Is fishing snow in lonely boat.

Liu Zongyuan (773–819) was a writer, philosopher, proser and thinker in the Tang Dynasty. Together with Han Yu, he supported Classical Prose Movement and was ranked among the "Eight Great Prose Masters of the Tang and Song Dynasties". He wrote numerous poems with steep style, nearly 100 proses with strong arguments and satire, and many travel notes with beautiful sceneries to express his inner feelings. He left *Mr. Hedong Anthology*.

京畿瑞雪图（局部） 唐代 李思训
Snow Scene in the Capital City and Its Environs (partial), Tang Dynasty, Li Sixun

崔 护 Cui Hu

题都城南庄

去年今日此门中,
人面桃花相映红。
人面不知何处去,
桃花依旧笑春风。

WRITTEN IN A VILLAGE SOUTH OF THE CAPITAL

In this house on this day last year, a pink face vied
In beauty with the pink peach blossoms side by side.
I do not know today where the pink face has gone;
In vernal breeze still smile pink peach blossoms full-blown.

Cui Hu served as an official in the Tang Dynasty. He was also a poet and created various graceful and restrained poems. Among his only six existing works which were included in *Quan Tang Shi* (*Complete Tang Poem*), his poem entitled Written in a Village South of the Capital is one of the most recognizable, bringing his immortal reputation.

捣练图（局部） 唐代 张萱
Court Ladies Preparing Newly-Woven Silk (partial), Tang Dynasty, Zhang Xuan

萧翼赚兰亭图（局部） 唐代 阎立本
Xiaoyi Cheating Wang Xizhi's Calligraphic Work (Titled Preface to the Collection of Poems Composed at the Orchid Pavilion, partial), Tang Dynasty, Yan Liben

元 稹 Yuan Zhen

离思

曾经沧海难为水，
除却巫山不是云。
取次花丛懒回顾，
半缘修道半缘君。

THINKING OF MY DEAR DEPARTED

No water's wide enough when you have crossed the sea;
No cloud is beautiful but that which crowns the peak.
I pass by flowers which fail to attract poor me
Half for your sake and half for Taoism I seek.

Yuan Zhen (779–831) as an official was both promoted to be a chancellor and demoted to a remote area. He was clever and smart in his youth. He passed the Jinji level of imperial examination, together with Bai Juyi. Since then, they became friends and initiated New *Yuefu* Movement. He often wrote love and mourning poems, and was prominent for describing the love between a man and a woman in detail and vividly.

高逸图（局部） 唐代 孙位
Stories of Seven Sages of the Bamboo Grove (partial), Tang Dynasty, Sun Wei

贾 岛 Jia Dao

访隐者不遇

松下问童子，言师采药去。
只在此山中，云深不知处。

For an Absent Recluse

I ask your lad 'neath a pine tree.
"My master's gone for herbs," says he.
You hide amid the mountains proud,
I know not where deep in the cloud.

Jia Dao (779–843) was renowned for his bitter styled poems. When his capability and talent was spotted by Han Yu, he spent time learning from him until he planned a career in the court after his imperial examination. Unfortunately, he failed in many examinations. He excelled in five-character poems, which express his dissatisfaction and sufferings based on desolate and lonely sceneries. Together with Meng Jiao, he was recognized for the forcefulness and harshness of his poems. The *Changjiang Anthology* was written by him.

侍马图 唐代 佚名
A Horse and a Groom, Tang Dynasty, Anonymous

李 绅 Li Shen

悯农二首

（一）

春种一粒粟，
秋收万颗子。
四海无闲田，
农夫犹饿死。

（二）

锄禾日当午，
汗滴禾下土。
谁知盘中餐，
粒粒皆辛苦。

THE PEASANTS

I

Each seed that's sown in spring
Will make autumn yields high.
What will fertile fields bring?
Of hunger peasants die.

II

At noon they weed with hoes;
Their sweat drips on the soil.
Each bowl of rice, who knows?
Is the fruit of hard toil.

Li Shen (772–846) lost his father when he was a child. He served as an official after passing the Jinji level of imperial examination. He had close relationship with Yuan Zhen and Bai Juyi. As a supporter of New *Yuefu* Movement, he wrote 20 works in *Yuefu* style, which didn't pass down to generations. His *Zhuixiyou Anthology* (Three volumes) and *Miscellaneous Poetry* (One Volume) have been included into *Quan Tang Shi* (Complete Tang Poem).

簪花仕女图（局部） 唐代 周昉
Court Ladies Wearing Flowered Headdresses (partial), Tang Dynasty, Zhou Fang

杜 牧 Du Mu

过华清宫

长安回望绣成堆，
山顶千门次第开。
一骑红尘妃子笑，
无人知是荔枝来。

THE SUMMER PALACE

Viewed from afar, the hill's paved with brocades in piles;
The palace doors on hilltops opened one by one.
A steed which raised red dust won the fair mistress' smiles.
How many steeds which brought her fruit died on the run!

Du Mu (803–852) was a poet in later Tang Dynasty. His father served as a chancellor and he passed Jinji level of imperial examination after which he worked as an official. Together with Li Shangyin, he was an accomplished poet of that time, with his poem mainly depicting history in a majestic style, sometime beautiful and vivid landscapes. He was known as "Litter Du" (while "Big Du referred to Du Fu"). The *Fanchuan Anthology* is one of his works.

杜 牧 Du Mu

江南春

千里莺啼绿映红，
水村山郭酒旗风。
南朝四百八十寺，
多少楼台烟雨中。

Spring on the Southern Rivershore

Orioles sing for miles 'mid red blooms and green trees;
By hills and rills wineshop streamers wave in the breeze.
Four hundred eighty splendid temples still remain
Of Southern Dynasties in the mist and the rain.

海天旭日图（局部） 唐代 李昭道（宋摹本）
The Morning Sun over the Sea (partial), Tang Dynasty, Li Zhaodao (Copy of the Song Dynasty)

杜 牧 Du Mu

赤壁

折戟沉沙铁未销，
自将磨洗认前朝。
东风不与周郎便，
铜雀春深锁二乔。

THE RED CLIFF

We dig out broken halberds buried in the sand
And wash and rub these relics of an ancient war.
Had the east wind refused General Zhou a helping hand,
His foe'd have locked his fair wife on northern shore.

北齐校书图卷（局部） 唐代 阎立本
Scholars with Thoughtful Reflections in the Northern Qi Dynasty (partial), Tang Dynasty, Yan Liben

杜 牧 Du Mu

泊秦淮

烟笼寒水月笼沙，
夜泊秦淮近酒家。
商女不知亡国恨，
隔江犹唱《后庭花》。

MOORED ON RIVER QINHUAI

Cold water and sand bars veiled in misty moonlight,
I moor on River Qinhuai near wineshops at night.
The songstress knows not the grief of the captive king,
By riverside she sings his song of *Parting Spring*.

北齐校书图卷（局部）
Scholars with Thoughtful Reflections in the Northern Qi Dynasty (partial)

杜 牧 Du Mu

山行

远上寒山石径斜,
白云生处有人家。
停车坐爱枫林晚,
霜叶红于二月花。

Snow along the Yangtze River (partial), Tang Dynasty, Wang Wei

Going up the Hill

A slanting stony path leads far to the cold hill;
Where fleecy clouds are born, there appear cots and bowers.
I stop my cab at maple woods to gaze my fill;
Frost-bitten leaves look redder than early spring flowers.

江皋会遇图（局部） 唐代 王维
Meeting by the River (partial), Tang Dynasty, Wang Wei

温庭筠　Wen Tingyun

商山早行

晨起动征铎，客行悲故乡。
鸡声茅店月，人迹板桥霜。
槲叶落山路，枳花明驿墙。
因思杜陵梦，凫雁满回塘。

EARLY DEPARTURE

At dawn I rise and my cab bells begin
To ring, but in thoughts of home I am lost.
The cock crows as the moon sets o'er thatched inn;
Footprints are left on wood bridge paved with frost.
The mountain path is covered with oak leaves;
The posthouse bright with blooming orange trees.
The dream of my homeland last night still grieves:
A pool of mallards playing with wild geese.

Wen Tingyun (812?–866) lived an unconstrained life after failing in Jinji level of imperial examination many times. He focused on writing poems themed women's love with flowery and delicate words, but a few of his works demonstrated some political circumstances. As one of the representative poets in the Five Dynasties and Ten Kingdoms period, who only kept a close eye on the love of women and men, Wen had a profound impact on poets in the Song Dynasty.

北齐校书图卷(局部) 唐代 阎立本
Scholars with Thoughtful Reflections in the Northern Qi Dynasty (partial),
Tang Dynasty, Yan Liben

李商隐　Li Shangyin

锦瑟

锦瑟无端五十弦，一弦一柱思华年。
庄生晓梦迷蝴蝶，望帝春心托杜鹃。
沧海月明珠有泪，蓝田日暖玉生烟。
此情可待成追忆，只是当时已惘然。

THE SAD ZITHER

Why should the sad zither have fifty strings?
Each string, each strain evokes but vanished springs:
Dim morning dream to be a butterfly;
Amorous heart poured out in cuckoo's cry.
In moonlit pearls see tears in mermaid's eyes;
With sunburned mirth let blue jade vaporise.
Such feeling cannot be recalled again;
It seemed long lost e'en when it was felt then.

Li Shangyin (813?–858?) was among the few poets who deliberately pursued poetic beauty in the late Tang Dynasty and even the whole Tang Dynasty. He was renowned for his historical and unnamed poems with regulated rhymes, typical style, and various allusions for implied or ironic purposes. *Li Yishan Anthology* is one of his works.

李商隐 Li Shangyin

乐游原

向晚意不适,
驱车登古原。
夕阳无限好,
只是近黄昏。

On the Plain of Tombs

At dusk my heart is filled with gloom;
I drive my cab to ancient tomb.
The setting sun seems so sublime,
But it is near its dying time.

仙山楼观图卷（局部） 唐代 李昭道（传）
Fairy Mountains and Buildings (partial), Tang Dynasty, Li Zhaodao (purported)

人物故事图（局部） 唐代 周昉（传）
Figures and Stories (partial), Tang Dynasty, Zhou Fang (purported)

李商隐　Li Shangyin

夜雨寄北

君问归期未有期，
巴山夜雨涨秋池。
何当共剪西窗烛，
却话巴山夜雨时。

WRITTEN ON A RAINY NIGHT TO MY WIFE IN THE NORTH

You ask me when I can return, but I don't know;
It rains in western hills and autumn pool o'erflow.
When can we trim by window side the candlelight
And talk about the western hills in rainy night?

龙舟竞渡图（局部） 唐代 李昭道
Dragon Boat Racing (partial), Tang Dynasty, Li Zhaodao

李商隐 Li Shangyin

无题

昨夜星辰昨夜风，画楼西畔桂堂东。
身无彩凤双飞翼，心有灵犀一点通。
隔座送钩春酒暖，分曹射覆蜡灯红。
嗟余听鼓应官去，走马兰台类转蓬。

TO ONE UNNAMED

As last night twinkle stars, as last night blows the breeze
West of the painted bower, east of Cassia Hall.
Having no wings, I can't fly to you as I please;
Our hearts at one, your ears can hear my inner call.
Maybe you're playing hook in palm and drinking wine
Or guessing what the cup hides under candle red.
Alas! I hear the drum call me to duties mine;
Like rootless weed to Orchid Hall I ride ahead.

竹图 唐代 荥阳
Bamboos, Tang Dynasty, Rong Yang

李商隐 Li Shangyin

无题

相见时难别亦难,东风无力百花残。
春蚕到死丝方尽,蜡炬成灰泪始干。
晓镜但愁云鬓改,夜吟应觉月光寒。
蓬山此去无多路,青鸟殷勤为探看。

To One Unnamed

It's difficult for us to meet and hard to part;
The east wind is too weak to revive flowers dead.
Spring silkworm till its death spins silk from lovesick heart;
Candles only when burned up have no tears to shed.
At dawn I'm grieved to think your mirrored hair turns grey;
At night you would feel cold while I croon by moonlight.
To the three fairy hills it is not a long way.
Would the blue birds oft fly to see you on the height!

A Lady Gazing at the Moon by the River (partial), Tang Dynasty, Wu Daozi

李商隐　Li Shangyin

嫦娥

云母屏风烛影深，
长河渐落晓星沉。
嫦娥应悔偷灵药，
碧海青天夜夜心。

TO THE MOON GODDESS

Upon the marble screen the candlelight is winking;
The Silver River slants and morning stars are sinking.
You'd regret to have stolen the miraculous potion:
Each night you brood o'er the lonely celestial ocean.